Jersey Pines Ink

Presents

# A Little Fantasy Everywhere

**An Anthology**

**Edited by Dina Leacock**

JERSEY PINES INK

Interior Design— River Cove Productions

Cover art—Dar Albert, Wicked Smart Designs

Copyright © 2024 Jersey Pines Ink

ISBN: 978-1-948899-26-0

## Dedication

To all the fantasy creatures who always
help me get through life.

# To My Readers

It is my pleasure to publish this anthology through all the trials and delays. I am very proud of the final product and all the authors in this book.

Some of the stories were sent by authors using British-style English. I have decided to honor those differences.

I appreciate all the work that the authors of the stories have put into this book and am pleased to have so many international authors represented.

Thank you for all the work that everyone put into this book.

I hope as you read this book, you enjoy every story.


Dina Leacock

# A Little Fantasy Everywhere

**Stories of wonder that will make you smile and sometimes shiver.**

JERSEY PINES INK

# Table of Contents

# Table of Contents

# A Normal Life

## *Jill Hand*

The woman was back again. She had turned up the day before, asking to use the restroom. Jen let her, despite being under strict orders from Luis, owner of the EZ Grab Snaks 'N Stuff, not to allow just anyone to use the restroom. Luis had informed her that the restroom was for customers and employees only. Any transgression of this rule would be dealt with harshly.

"Meth-heads and junkies are always trying to get into the restroom. If they puke in there, I don't like it. If they die in there, I *really* don't like it. So nobody but customers who ain't junkies or meth-heads get to use the restroom, understand?"

Jen said she understood, although she wondered how she was supposed to distinguish those who intended to use the restroom for legitimate purposes from those who didn't. She wasn't a cop, or a drug counselor; she was a seventeen-year-old girl who worked at a crappy convenience store. Nevertheless, she let the woman use the restroom, even though she looked like she was homeless. Her tired eyes, greasy hair, and ragged jeans all screamed homelessness.

Jen felt sorry for her, and so she violated Luis' restroom rule. She had been relieved when the woman neither puked nor died, but simply left after a couple of minutes, giving Jen a shy smile and a mumbled, "Thanks."

And now she was back. Jen saw her sitting on the curb in the parking lot and groaned. The woman would ask passersby for spare change, a cigarette, or, God forbid, she would proposition the male customers. Luis would lose his mind if the EZ Grab became known as a place where easy grabbing of a sexual nature took place.

Luis had come to this country with nothing but the clothes on his back, as he frequently reminded Jen and the other people who were unfortunate enough to be in his employ. He had worked hard to become a successful businessman, he said, sounding like Jeff Bezos and not the owner of a shabby convenience store. If he could do it without government handouts, then so could anyone. Unless they were lazy freeloaders who didn't want to work, he'd add darkly.

As Jen watched, the woman rose from the curb and walked toward the door.

*Oh, damn! Here she comes! I let her use the restroom and now she's targeted me as an easy mark,* Jen thought, panicked. Would the woman ask her for money, of if she could buy a single cigarette? Selling "loosies," as they were known, was strictly forbidden by law, and by Luis.

Jen braced herself.

"Hi, I was wondering if you'd give me a drink," the woman said.

For a moment Jen thought the woman meant a drink of alcohol, but then she saw she was looking at the bottled water in the cooler case.

"Water? Sure, okay," Jen said, relieved that it was all the woman wanted. Luis had bought several pallet-loads of bottled water during the Covid pandemic. There were plenty left over. Jen was allowed to take one bottle and one plastic-wrapped sandwich during her shift. She'd give a bottle of water to the homeless woman and Luis would be none the wiser.

"I can't pay for it," the woman said, looking down at the floor.

"Not a problem. Here, have a sandwich, too."

"Really?"

"Yeah, take one, and the water."

The woman smiled, displaying surprisingly white teeth. "You're a peach. Listen, if you could have anything, anything at all, what would you wish for?"

No one had ever asked her that before, but Jen didn't even have to think.

"A normal life," she said.

The woman smiled again. "Really? And what would that consist of?

"A nice house, not a mansion, but a house that was clean and where I wouldn't be ashamed to invite my friends over. Plus a mom who wasn't a drunk and a dad who lived with us and not in Kentucky or wherever he is now and who has a job and remembers my birthday."

Jen was surprised to see tears in the woman's eyes.

"That's a good wish, Jen. Thanks for the water and the sandwich."

3

It wasn't until after the woman left that Jen realized she hadn't mentioned her name, but then she remembered she was wearing a name tag that said HELLO! MY NAME IS JEN. HOW CAN I HELP?

Of course, that's how the woman knew her name.

The SUV pulled in when Jen's shift ended. A woman got out. She looked vaguely familiar, but Jen couldn't place her. Then she realized, with astonishment, that it was her mom. It wasn't the version of her mom she had seen that morning, passed out on the living room couch, an empty bottle of vodka on the floor beside her. This was a version of her mom with clear eyes and a nice haircut.

"Honey, did you have a nice day? How was school?"

For a moment, Jen was speechless. "Mom? Where did you get that SUV? You're not supposed to be driving."

"Sweetheart, are you okay? I've had that SUV for three years, remember? And why shouldn't I be driving? Her mother's forehead creased with concern. "Is your blood sugar low? Here, have a peppermint."

Her mom opened her purse – a stylish purse, not the beat-up one she usually carried – and handed her a wrapped peppermint. "Dad's making burgers on the grill," she said.

Jen felt dazed, as if she'd stepped into an alternate reality. "Dad? Isn't he in Kentucky?"

Her mother looked puzzled. "Why would he be in Kentucky? He's home, like always. That is, when he's not at the office, or playing golf."

Her father played golf? That was news to Jen.

"After dinner, let's go over your college applications. How does that sound?"

Jen breathed a silent thank-you to the woman who had granted her wish.

"It sounds good," she said.

# How to Tell Apart Gothinians and Gordinians

## Jonathan Reddoch

How does one tell apart members on the Gothinian and Gordinian races? They have similar mild complexions. Their fingernails are both short and green. They have blueish or yellow hair that shines in the starlight. They have long pointed ears, perfect for hearing the faintest footfall.

How then can you distinguish these two striking groups of extraordinary denizens within the Realm Worthitia?

Not by their physical features I assure you. And while it may be tempting to make assumptions based on their garb (Gothinian blue and scarlet Gordinian liveries) this is only sometimes the case; they often wear corporal grey or purple satin or humble brown depending on their taste and region and family wealth.

As for speech, it is said Gordinians speak with the frenzy of a million bustling gentlebees and the Gothinians with the smooth tongue of golden slothbears rising and falling with each long breath. However, this is only a stereotype based on urban versus rural culture.

So, what is the true answer?

You must ask the right question!

*Where does the world end and eternity begin?*

This is the question that has plagued the Gothinians for centuries beyond measure. To answer it is their singular philosophical purpose. And when presented with such an inquiry Gothinians will respond with a long pause, so long that you may have forgotten you had even asked it by the time they open their mouths again to answer. And when they do, they will recite a proverb followed by a mile-long sigh.

*Lasoute jghite 'jik-leeebhour*
*Poushidzur furghuther snouur*

The verse, mind you, is not in any discernable language. The Gothinians have no understanding of the words they speak. In fact, there is even a much-heated debate about the accurate pronunciation and spelling. One popular theory posits that it is the language of the fallen septic gods. Others claim it is merely gibberish.

The answer to the riddle is not found on the lips, or inside the brain. It is not written in a book or whispered in the ear. The meaning of the answer echoes from the distant past. The answer lies not here nor there, but on the road, the blind road that leads to the edge of the world and the first faith-filled step off it into eternity.

And if you ask a Gordinian the same riddle?

They are equally likely to tell you in their native tongue to "drop off the edge of the unknown world and map the bottom with your arse."

Alternatively, if you prefer an easier way discern to their identity, simply ask for a cookie. Gothinians are abysmal bakers (they get distracted and always burn their batch) but Gordinian double-doodles are a true confectionary delight.

# GREMLINS

## *Eddie Spohn*

After a sleepless night of waiting for Ryan to come home, Jen rolled out of bed and went to the kitchen to boil some water for tea. The sun had risen a short time ago, filling the windows with a bright yellowness promising another day of record-breaking heat. Jen peered out across the front yard to the driveway where her Honda was parked. The spot where Ryan placed his prized Dodge Charger was empty.

Of course it was empty. That car was an extension of him, part of his identity, his mechanical lover. It was the Charger he sped off in whenever things got too hectic at home.

*How convenient,* she thought. *Another Friday night argument where he leaves because he needs to cool off.*

Jen did not remember what the argument had been about. The origins were never really clear. It always seemed as if he was *pushing* for them. On the weekends, their conversations were like a minefield where Jen never knew where to step, because the slightest thing could trigger his anger.

9

It was confusing, maddening, and Ryan assured her it was all her fault. Everything was. And she was lucky to have him. Lucky to have someone who would put up with her crazy instability. Forgive a guy for needing some time away.

When the tea kettle whistled Jen poured the boiling liquid into a cup containing two bags of chai. She walked out into the backyard, blowing onto the surface of the tea to cool it down enough for that first sip.

She paused just outside the door. The lid of their wheeled propane barbeque grill was flipped open. Bundles of plucked wildflowers were stuck into the grease-crusted cooking grates in between rows of pebbles from the nearby lake. Like something a mischievous child would do.

*Or a drunk Ryan.*

Because as foul tempered as he could be, the pendulum of his moods could also swing the other way. He could broadside her with an unexpected thoughtful gift or romantic gesture, so seemingly pure and open that her heart melted. A brief ray of sunshine in the eye of a storm, with no rhyme or reason to it. Something to be cherished while it lasted.

A round metal dining table was set beside the barbeque. The four chairs around it were upended with their legs facing skyward. They had not been that way last night.

*Ryan,* she concluded, looking away into the distance. The backyard of the rental went all the way to the sandy shore of a wide kettle lake. The view of the sun rising over the water was majestic, the orange streak of reflected light broken up into a flurry of glittering gems. The image helped elevate her otherwise melancholy mood. Such a shame she was always alone when she saw it.

She made her slow way down towards the shore. She was aware of a disturbance in the woods around her. Hoots and chirps of some animals. She saw them in the shadowy undergrowth, miniature bipedal things with big round heads, pointy ears and long tails, rushing about in agitation along the dark edge of the woods. They seemed to be afraid of the sunlight and would not venture out from the cover of the undergrowth. She could make out no details of them except for their strange silhouettes and the occasional glint of sunlight on wide nocturnal eyes.

*Raccoons,* Jen thought with alarm, thinking that was the only animal fitting what she was seeing. And with that was the worry over something she had heard somewhere about rabid raccoons being the only ones out during the day.

She took two steps back as something squeaked nearer to her. Out in the center of the yard was a small clump of purple coneflowers growing next to a knee-high boulder. One of the creatures from the woods, this one much smaller, hid within an ever shrinking patch of shadow underneath some foliage and against the base of the boulder. It was terrified, staring out from the shadows with wide eyes as shiny as the lake surface, emitting shrill cries that brought the creatures in the woods to heights of frenzy. Yet none of them dared cross the yard to rescue it, and it was frozen in place uttering its pitiful wails.

*It's a baby stuck out in the open,* Jen surmised. She had a relatively clear view of the stranded youngling and saw it was neither rabid nor raccoon. She slowly got down on her hands and knees to better inspect the creature. Her motion brought it and the others to renewed hysterics, and it cowered but could not retreat without being exposed to direct sunlight.

"Easy," she said gently. "I'm not going to hurt you."

Jen reached very slowly into the pool of darkness with one opened hand and touched the shivering creature atop its head. The ones in the woods shrieked at this, but the little one itself merely shivered and mewled. Its fur was soft and warm and Jen carefully slipped her palm beneath it. "Easy," she said, slowly bringing it out of its hiding place, careful to block the sunlight with her body. The creatures grew suddenly quiet, understanding Jen meant no harm.

She cupped the creature to her stomach, shielded from the sun, and brought it to the closest tree line, setting the creature down in the dark undergrowth. Before scampering away, the little one deposited a piece of metal in her palm. Jen looked at the object with a smile on her face, the woods resounding with sounds of happy reunion.

It was one of the skull valve covers from Ryan's car. He'd been accusing her of taking them and letting the air out of his tires for spite.

"You little rascals," Jen muttered at the now silent woods.

———————

Ryan came back that evening, close to midnight.

"Where've you been?" Jen asked. "A call would have been nice."

Ryan looked haggard from partying. "A call would have been nice," he mocked. "Did you worry about *me?* No, all you did was leave messages asking when I was coming home. I could have been dead and all you'd have done is accuse me of cheating on you. I feel like this is a prison sentence." He angrily stuffed fresh clothes into a carry bag in preparation for one of his less than graceful exits. The old Ryan *bounce*.

He paused in the midst of the procedure and tossed the bag onto the floor. He raised one hand and pointed the index finger at Jen. "And another thing. Stop messing with my car. I know it's you playing around with my tires. You think letting the air out of them is going to stop me from going anywhere? I have an air pump. Remember? You bought it for me for my birthday."

This was followed by a loud ten minutes of argument, most of it in Ryan's angry basso, ending in him storming from the house with the carry bag clenched in one hand. Jen did not chase him. She sat on the edge of their bed sobbing, blaming herself for the whole thing.

Outside the Charger's hemi motor roared to life. The car tore off in a squeal of tires.

Ryan sped down the dark mountain road. Despite the speed, the motor seemed to be losing power. It gurgled and sputtered, and he thought, *Oh, you did it now, Jen. This is the last straw.*

Only sugar in the gas tank would do something like this. Come to think of it, he could smell gasoline now, coming in waves through the air vents and giving him an instant headache. He let off the accelerator and switched to the brake, intending to turn around and teach Jen why only mechanics should touch cars. And why she should never touch *his*.

The brake pedal gave no resistance and sank to the floor. The car did not slow down at all. There was a sudden hollow boom and the vehicle shook as the front hood whipped open and spun skyward off its hinges. Billows of flame roared off the superheated engine, fed by a constant stream of gasoline spurting from a ruptured fuel line. More like a *torn out* fuel line.

To match the torn out brake lines.

Ahead, a curve in the road approached all too quickly. Ryan saw it through the orange sheet of flame dancing over the windshield. His instinct was to bail from the vehicle, but things happened at light speed, and even as the thought was born it was already too late. The Charger left the road, sailing off an embankment towards the rocky ground fifty feet below, cutting through the darkness like a meteor.

The explosive punchline brought the laughing audience to its furry knees.

# THE EMPTY HOUSE

## *Ed Ahern*

The little house was empty for two months. Charles had lived alone there, and he died there as well, softly gasping in a morphine coma. He roused just enough to see me and whisper, "Take care of Agatha." I tried to ask  she was, but he'd lapsed back into a stupor.

I'd agreed, despite misgivings, to be his executor. I'd already gathered the necessary information on financial assets, real estate and personal property, but the estate proceeds were being contested and all I could do was watch from the sidelines while relatives and charities bickered.

Meanwhile, I visited the house every other day to recover stray mail and check that the gas, electricity and water still flowed without interruption or leak. A house without people develops an echoey loneliness that's hard to describe but easy to sense. Its mission thwarted, it gently degenerates, dust settling into patina. The food long disposed of, the important records extracted like teeth, the purposeless, worn furniture was left behind in memorial.

One breezy spring afternoon I was rechecking financial and tax records in the second bedroom Charles used as a den office. The house's grime and slowly flaking paint were imperceptibly worse, but I got a vague apprehension that someone had been or still was in the house. I checked all the outside doors and rooms, but nothing was missing, unlocked or moved, and no intruder appeared. And yet it felt like someone had disturbed the emptiness. I sat back down.

Bright sunlight streamed through dirty windows into rooms in bad need of use or emptying. The dust motes swirled only when I moved. But I felt not alone. It wasn't the specter of Charles, that curmudgeonly bachelor had a much different tone while living and presumably kept it while dead. It felt different, lighter and yet more melancholy than Charles had been.

I perched in the office chair without focus, diverting myself with misgivings about the greedy living. After five minutes, feeling like an idiot, I stood up to leave. And in the doorway dust motes swirled. I sat back down.

The motes, glinting in the sun, jittered over to a small love seat and paused. The frumpy room seemed to hold a presence. I stifled the flip urge to introduce myself and kept waiting. In that passive, receptive state I smelled gardenias. Impossible, of course, because the unwatered house plants had been dead for weeks.

I felt that awkward social pause of two strangers waiting for the other to speak. I gave in to momentary insanity. "Charles has been dead for a while, you may as well move on."

The motes danced in some undetected waft of air. There was no real shape to them, but I thought I saw a middle-aged woman, worn down until the fine points were exposed. A stray thought wandered in. "Agatha?"

The dust particles bounced more vigorously.

"Okay, Agatha." I wondered if I'd been drugged somehow, but I continued. "He's gone, Agatha. You'll need to move along as well. You probably won't like the new occupants, whoever they'll be."

The faint cloud shimmered in the light. There felt like a pause, like a willing listener waiting for me to unburden myself. I'd tried to spare Beth, my wife of many years, from the acrimony surrounding the inheritances. I was being offered a chance to do so, even if just to myself.

"I'm guessing you know Charles. No immediate family, but several grasping second cousins whom he disliked and ignored while he was alive."

The motes settled into a rhythm, like breaths or beach waves. The gardenia scent was stronger, almost overwhelming the funky, stale clothes smell of the house.

"They want to rip apart his will, ignore his specific directions and divvy up the pile. And I'm the ignorant champion of a dead man."

In the angled afternoon light, the swirl seemed to tighten and intensify. I blathered on for another ten minutes and when I stopped I felt better. The resonance of my harsh words had calmed me, and I left to go home.

I returned that next morning, but the light was wrong, and I couldn't discern any air movement. I came back that same afternoon to discover that it hadn't been a fluke, that the dust particles were perceptibly swaying. I shifted into my anxieties about being an executor and when finished felt relieved, revealing my concerns to a mother confessor who didn't require penance.

From then on, I visited the house almost daily, gradually switching from Charles' situation to my own, revealing my personal angers and fears. The experience was cathartic. Beth became concerned, asking if I wasn't fixating on the house and poor dead Charles. I tried, unsuccessfully, to assure her that I was diligently working on estate matters, but she merely nodded and allowed me the aberration.

After almost a year of wrangling and judicial pronouncements, the cousins left frustrated, and Charles' wishes were confirmed. I was able to schedule the sell-off of the assets, and braced myself to say goodbye.

That last early spring afternoon, I went to Charles' house. Agatha was waiting. I blurted it out as soon as I sat down. "I have bad news. This house, your home, was sold to a company that will tear it down and put in a zero-lot line mini-McMansion. You'll be homeless. I'm so sorry."

The motes appeared to tighten into cordage, and then, like an exhale, wafted toward me. I felt, I thought I felt, a light touch on my hand, as if it were being patted. Then the dust dissipated and drifted away.

I locked up and went home. Beth was already there. "Are you finally done with that house? Maybe now we can spend some time together."

As I plopped into my recliner and picked up the remote, I glimpsed a swirl of air disturbing plant leaves in the corner, and smelled gardenia. "Maybe," I said.

# Unwelcome Exposure

## *Rachel Dib*

"You revealed yourself again!"

Carl lowered his chin, his eyes downcast. He dragged a prehensile foot in a series of arches, creating a rainbow in the detritus. "It was an accident. I thought they were all out."

Ranger Joe shook his head. "It's always an accident with you, Carl. It's always, 'Oh, I didn't know anyone was using that campsite,' or 'But the people were laughing so hard, I couldn't resist peeking at what was so funny,' or—and this one is my favorite—'But they had hotdogs.'"

"I love hotdogs," Carl grumbled.

Ignoring the utterance, Ranger Joe continued. "At least those times, people only glimpsed you. No one could definitively prove your existence." He crossed his arms and glared up his nose at the sasquatch. "This time, that twelve-year-old you so gleefully waved at snapped a *picture*!"

"Stupid pocket phones," the sasquatch muttered.

"They're called cell phones, Carl. I've explained this."

Carl rolled his eyes. "And I've told *you* 'cell phone' doesn't make any sense. You keep them in your pocket. Not a cell." He motioned toward Ranger Joe's khakis. "Yours is in your pocket right now."

"As I've explained before, it has to do with towers and networks. Not where you keep it. Also, not the point." Ranger Joe waved his hands as if clearing the air. "Long story short, because of that picture, a raucous search party is scouring the forest looking for the legendary Bigfoot."

"I hate that name." Carl glanced down at his feet. "They're not that big. But even if they were, it's rude to point it out. What if I called your kind—"

"Carl, focus." Ranger Joe snapped his fingers. "This is a real problem."

"I don't see why. Your kind has taken pictures of me before." He shrugged. "Nothing happened."

"True." Ranger Joe nodded. Then he slipped his phone from his pocket, illuminated the screen, and shoved the device in Carl's ape-like face. "But were the pictures ever this clear?"

Carl studied the phone screen. His caramel eyes brightened, and his thick lips turned upward in a goofy grin. "He got my good side!"

"No, Carl," Ranger Joe growled. "He got your *face*! A pixel perfect picture of your *entire* face!"

"Still a good picture."

Ranger Joe clicked his tongue. "It is a good picture, Carl. And therein lies the problem. It's *too* good a picture." He sighed. "I'm sorry, but you're going to have to leave the area for a while."

Nodding slowly, the sasquatch blew out his cheeks. "I

guess I can go to...What was it? Oheeo? Be 'the Grassman' for a while."

"It's Ohio, and you hid out there last month after you shared hotdogs with that camper."

"Oh yeah. He was nice." Carl's brow furrowed. "Or he was until he wrote about me on your pocket phone. We had an understanding. That night was to stay between us. In fact, he claimed he didn't even know you."

"And he doesn't. I found the story of that little mishap posted online."

Carl blinked. "On what line?"

"Don't worry about it. The point is, you can't go be the Grassman."

Pursing his lips, Carl absentmindedly snapped a small branch from a nearby tree and started plucking off its leaves. "Then I'll go be Momo. Haven't been that in a while."

"Nope. Every time you head to Missouri, you get distracted. I can't chance you going astray and disappearing somewhere random right now."

Carl blew a raspberry. "I won't get distracted."

"Yeah?" Ranger Joe tilted his head. "My records indicate you haven't successfully made it back to Missouri since the seventies."

"So."

"That's over fifty years ago, Carl."

"Oh." The sasquatch grinned impishly and wagged a bushy brow. "I won't get distracted if you come with me."

"I can't accompany you, Carl." Ranger Joe sighed. "I have to stay here and ensure a drunken search party doesn't burn down the forest and create other such mayhem."

"Fine. If I can't be the Grassman or Momo, I'll go be with the virgins and become their Wood Booger again."

Ranger Joe shook his head. "They're called Virginians and that's too close to here. You need to travel farther south. *Much* farther south."

The sasquatch tensed, clutching his branch a little tighter. He narrowed his eyes. "You don't mean..."

Ranger Joe smirked. "Oh, but I do."

"But there's swamps." Carl grimaced, exposing a set of large, yellowed teeth. "I hate swamps."

"Then don't step in one."

"And there's gators." Carl gave a disgruntled sniff. "They may taste good, but they're grumpy. One tried to bite my foot."

Ranger Joe flung out a dismissive hand. "Well, unless you're hungry, stay away from alligators too."

"But the residents call me *Skunk Ape*!" Carl whined. "That doesn't even make any sense."

"And your other names do?" Ranger Joe lifted a brow.

Carl wrinkled his nose. "At least my other names don't imply that I stink."

"It's hot and humid down there. After a week of hanging out in the everglades, you probably *do* stink," Ranger Joe pointed out. "But hey, if you don't want to go to Florida, Ranger Lou is taking a trip abroad soon. It'd be an extended vacation, but I can ask him to bring you along. He'll understand the urgency of the matter."

Carl's small ears perked in interest. "Australia? I've always wanted to meet a Yowie."

"Not this time. He's flying to Asia." Ranger Joe's lip quirked.

"In fact, he'll be near the Himalayas. I'm sure he'll drop you off if you want to visit your Yeti friend."

"You know Raj and I aren't speaking right now." Carl scowled.

"Oh right. You made fun of his new hairstyle a few years back."

"If he didn't want to look like a giant cotton ball, he shouldn't have used a pick on his hair."

"Hmm." Ranger Joe shrugged. "Well, it's either reconcile with Raj or..."

Carl growled, barring his teeth. "I'll be the Skunk Ape."

Ranger Joe smiled. "I'll help you pack."

# THE DRAGONLADY'S SMILE

## *Teel James Glenn*

The Dragonlady was tall, stunning and raven-haired with an eyepatch and an attitude, exactly the kind of woman that fed into all my dysfunctional wiring and drove me crazy. She would mess with my mind by alternating the eyepatch on different days and gave me a conspiratorial smirk when I noticed.

I stopped by the tent she hawked in front of every morning on my security rounds before the public was allowed onto the renaissance faire grounds. I tried my considerable charm on the Dragonnlady but all I ever got was that maddening, enticing smile.

"Step up," she bellowed in a fake Cornwall accent, "Step up, warm bloods, and see the awesome sleeping dragon!" She stood on a wooden platform in front of the big canvas, circus type tent and cracked a six-foot bullwhip every once and a while for emphasis. "See the great reptile as he slumbers and see his golden hoard; just one dollar!"

She was barker and tour guide for the Sleeping Dragon exhibit, a jobbed-in show that rented the tent each year from the faire owners and had two burly costumed 'dragon hunters' out front to collect its own cash each day.

The crowds filed in at a steady pace all day and exited around the back suitably impressed.

I'd seen the show the first weekend of the faire, when she had first caught my eye.

Just inside the entrance flap the tent was dark and smoky. The Dragonlady, suitably dressed in medieval leather garb, would lead in the crowd with a knowing smile and a wink. "Enter ye the Sleeping Dragon's den," she would intone in a solemn whisper. "But at your own risk for he guards his hoard like the greedy miser that he is and the great scaled beast slumbers but fitfully. Make no noise or I will not be responsible for what might occur!"

Then she led the crowd around an interior curtain to the main room of the tent to reveal the Sleeping Dragon.

It was impressive; the latex dragon puppet was a dull brown, twenty feet long (not counting the tail), had stiff ridge plates on its back and a long narrow beaked head. Its eyes were closed and it was curled up like a slumbering dog. It slept on and was surrounded by sacks of gold coins piled up artistically to create a comfy looking nest.

All the audience oohed and awed when tiny puffs of smoke would drift at irregular intervals from the beast's nostrils. The crowning bit of showmanship was the slow gentle rise and fall of the great saurian's chest as it slumbered; you could almost imagine the sound of it snoring.

"The beast rests here for the summer," the Dragonlady

said, with an expansive gesture, "but we have to hope he has no nightmares . . ."

The crowd shuffled slowly past the dragon, awed by the exacting detail of claws, scales and rough skin pores. Even lashes on the great closed eyelids of the beast.

At that moment the Dragonlady 'accidently' knocked over a tripod filled with coins that clattered to the carpet. Suddenly the dragon's eye flew open, and the great yellow orb focused on the audience.

Someone screamed and the crowd raced, giggling, out of the tent flap.

I hung back until the group had exited and got up close to my Dragonlady.

"Nice show there, Cyclops," I said.

She gave me that smile that made me all tingly and said in a quiet voice, "We aim to please, m'lord." She set up the tripod again and dropped coins into the bowl.

"Then why not meet me for a drink after the show tonight?"

"We don't aim to please that much, my warm blood." She winked with her un-patched eye. Before I could come up with a witty comeback, she hurried off to lead in the next group of paying customers.

So, it went the whole summer; every time I saw her we sparred verbally and I struck out. A guy could develop a complex, except that I found out I wasn't special: she had never dated anyone at the faire in the three years she had worked it.

No one could tell me where the Sleeping Dragon show was based out of or where they went when the show closed either, so I couldn't track down a clue about her real name.

If I was gonna solve the mystery of my Dragonlady I had

to do it by closing night party.

That closing night party came all too quick and by midnight my eyepatched siren had still not arrived. I was drunk and looking for her and had had more than my share of bottle dreams. All I could think of, even in the noise and bustle of the cast party, was my Dragonlady.

Rumor had it that the Sleeping Dragon show would be gone tomorrow and in my beer haze I was sure I'd die if I didn't see her again. I had to at least learn her name.

I slipped away from the party and down onto the grounds of the faire. I was pretty unsteady but eventually the dark shape of the Sleeping Dragon tent loomed before me.

There was no one in sight, and the front tent flap was laced closed, so I staggered to the edge of the tent and squirmed beneath the bottom of the canvas.

The inside of the tent was not the pitch black I expected, there was a faint flickering red glow that suggested a fire somewhere, but I couldn't locate it.

Even with the phantom glow it was hard to keep from tripping over sacks of coins and other vague shapes in the near dark. I couldn't see my sleek sinister lady but I could see the great saurian bulk, still pulsing with imitation respiration.

Then I saw her, standing across the tent with her back to me.

"Hey, Dragonlady," I called "Your Prince Charming is here." She didn't move so I staggered closer.

"Come on, mystery lady," I said, "Please give me a break; I gotta at least know your name."

She never turned to even acknowledge me as I navigated the coin sack maze over to her.

"Take pity on a vet, cupcake." I pleaded as I reached for her shoulder. The leather of her doublet was cool to the touch as I pulled her around to face me. I was a little unsteady and pulled too hard, so she fell over at me. I was taken by surprise but still caught her in my arms. She was so light.

And stiff.

"Hey, honey, you okay?" Her skin was cold to the touch and when I felt for pulse there was none.

I got scared.

"Oh geeze," I exclaimed. I knelt at her side, my besotted brain frantically trying to remember how to do CPR.

I reached down to touch her cheek and heard a sound from behind me unlike anything I had ever heard before. It was like the low rumbling of a thousand distant thunderclouds or the roar of an angry surf. I felt the hairs on the back of my neck stand on end.

The rumbling continued so I had no choice but to turn.

What I saw has been my stuff of nightmares since the Dragon stirred.

The great reptilian bulk rolled toward me, heaving up on its forelegs like a sleeper waking to his first stretch.

The huge-lidded eyes opened and stared directly at me.

I think I wet myself.

The beast rose to all fours and waggled its oversized head from side to side as if to work out a kink in its neck.

I was paralyzed with fear. I watched as the creature walked around the tent, pushing all the bags of coins into the center of the oriental carpet that served as floor to the space. Then it grabbed the four corners of the rug and bundled the contents like Santa's sack and threw it over its shoulder.

That got me moving, I grabbed my lady up in my arms and

backed toward the door flap, hoping the Dragon wouldn't look our way then something yanked the woman out of my arms, and I fell on my butt.

There was a cable that was wrapped around her right ankle. I reached down to free it and found something odd. It was attached directly to her boot.

Then the Dragon was right above me, its breath hot and oddly sweet. It reached a huge taloned hand toward us, grabbed the cable from the Dragonlady's heel and un-looped it to straighten it out.

Suddenly the Dragonlady sat up and turned her head to look at me and said, "silly warm blood."

I knew for certain that it wasn't her voice. "You really should not pay so much attention to surface details."

The simulcrum smiled and walked past me to climb into the carpet sack being held by the Dragon pulling the cable attached to her heel in behind her.

The Dragon reared up, reached above it to fold back a vent in the ceiling of the tent to expose the night sky above and unfurled its leathery wings. It looked down at me and spoke in a voice like the rumble of thunder.

"See you next year, Warmblood." It crouched and leapt upward with a single sweep of its wings. A hot sweet wind drove me to the ground where I passed out cold.

When I opened my eyes I was holding an eyepatch in my hand.

I never went back to that faire . . .

# LUCINDA

## Michael D. Burnside

Henry stepped out of his cabin and winced. The sun had begun to burn off the morning fog, leaving enough light to stab into his eyeballs. He'd been up late drinking to prove himself worthy to a group of fools. He paused to give his throbbing brain a moment to adjust. Before he turned away, he spotted a strange figure walking out of the mist.

Coming up the road was a girl marked by long blonde hair of such a light shade that it was almost silver. Her hair hung in disarray, matted on one side, showing she'd slept on the ground. She was tall and wore ill-fitting clothes that were too big for her. When she stopped in front of him, Henry found himself staring into ocean-blue eyes.

"How did you make it up that road?" asked Henry. "It's been besieged by bandits for weeks."

The girl glanced back down the road. "Yes, there were bandits. They stole everything I had, even my clothes." She tugged on her oversized shirt. "I managed to sneak into their camp and steal these."

Henry shook his head. "It's amazing you're alive. You're blessed to be so lucky. What's your name?"

"Lucinda, but you may call me Lucy."

"Well, Lucy. You look as if you've been out all night. May I buy you some breakfast? Perhaps some of your fortune will rub off on me."

Lucy's eyes lit up. "Would there happen to be sausages?"

Henry nodded. "That and some biscuits with a bit of ale to wash them down."

At the tavern, Lucy piled her plate full of mild sausages, passed by the biscuits, and gave no thought at all to the available greens.

Henry paid her tab, mostly because it was the hospitable thing to do, but partly because being seen with a pretty girl would raise his reputation, even if she was a bit disheveled at the moment. He sat across from her and watched in wonder as she ravenously devoured her breakfast.

Henry's focus on Lucy broke when Edward and his two sycophants—Theodore and Liam—entered the room. Despite the summer heat, Edward wore a blue waistcoat with shiny gold buttons. All of them wore white linen shirts and tan knee breeches with white stockings. The excessive drinking of the previous evening showed in their bloodshot eyes, but alarm had drawn their features tight. Spying Henry, they rushed to his table.

"Something terrible has happened on the western road," blurted Edward.

Liam locked his gaze on Lucy. "Who is this?" he demanded.

"Another bandit attack?" asked Henry, ignoring Liam's interruption.

"Some refugees from Bria, hoping the bandits weren't early-risers, risked the road this morning," said Edward. "They came across a mauled corpse. They followed multiple blood trails into the forest and found a camp strewn with bodies."

In between chews, Lucy muttered, "They followed a path of blood into bandit-filled woods?" She pointed a fork at Edward. "People from Bria are idiots." She went back to eating.

Startled by Lucy's comment, Edward paused a moment before continuing. "The bodies were torn apart." He leaned in closer and whispered. "The refugees say they saw the footprints of a werewolf."

Lucy raised an eyebrow. "Going to jump straight to the conclusion that it was a werewolf and not just a regular wolf?"

"A regular wolf wouldn't have attacked a group of well armed men," insisted Edward.

Lucy shrugged and downed another sausage.

"Was it even a full moon last night?" asked Henry.

Theodore, apparently excited that he had something to share, rushed forward. "No, but they say an experienced werewolf can control when they change."

Lucy gave Theodore a nod and he beamed in delight, which irritated Henry. "Who are *they*?" he asked.

Theodore hesitated before guessing, "Werewolf experts?"

"Who might possibly be werewolves themselves," added Lucy with a conspiratorial grin.

Edward put on a determined face and looked at Edward. "We're going to grab our muskets and hunt this thing down before it eats anyone else. Care to join us?"

Before Henry could respond, Lucy slammed her fist down on the table. She glared at Edward. "First off, no one said anyone had been eaten. No self-respecting werewolf is going to eat a collection of filthy bandits." She jabbed a finger at him. "Secondly, your plan is to hunt down the werewolf that took out the bandits that besieged your town for weeks. You couldn't deal with the bandits; what makes you think you have any chance against the werewolf that killed them?"

"Um..." stammered Edward.

"The spirit of our convictions?" offered Liam.

Lucy snorted. "Yes, 'Died for the spirit of their convictions' will look good on your tombstones."

"What do you suggest, then?" asked Edward.

"Make a deal with the werewolf," replied Lucy.

"A deal?" asked Edward incredulously. "With a monster?"

Lucy sighed. "You know, it was said that the folks in Bria had a werewolf. It offered to protect them, but did they take up the offer? No. They started melting down all their silver to make musket balls, so the werewolf left. And what happened? The whole city has been ravaged by pirates. Now, sure, you could drive off the werewolf by doing the same thing. You could also lay out all your valuables for the convenience of the pirates when they get around to following the refugees up the road."

Henry looked Lucy up and down. Edward, Liam, and Theodore followed Henry's eyes as they settled on the oversized sleeves of a shirt that clearly had not belonged to her until very recently.

Theodore took a step back from the table.

"Or?" asked Henry.

"You hire the werewolf to protect you," replied Lucy.

"And how do we know we can trust this werewolf?" asked Edward.

"Well, if she hasn't killed you by now, she probably doesn't intend to," answered Lucy.

"And how would we pay her?" asked Henry.

Lucy picked up a sausage and waved it in the air. "You already have."

# Roger and the Ghost

## *Paul Lonardo*

She heard the laughter of the trespassers as they made their way across the lawn. The two boys who mounted the steps to the front porch were not wearing costumes.

The pounding on the door rattled the interior wall, dislodging a layer of dust, which drifted down from the ceiling like dirty snowflakes.

"Trick or treat, Dead Girl," said the boy carrying two pillowcases full of candy.

She quickly ducked behind the couch when a shadow appeared in the window.

"I think I saw her!" the other boy screamed.

His silhouette filled the window as light from his cell phone failed to penetrate the pitch-black interior.

She was trapped. Her only hope was to make a run for it before the teens got inside. There was a large open space between her and the door in the kitchen that led to the basement. She was sure to be seen, but she had no choice. She dashed toward the kitchen, hoping the shadows would conceal her movement.

"There she is! Let's get her!"

As she entered the kitchen, the back door started to open. She remembered that she'd left it unlocked after coming in from the backyard earlier. She quickly dove under the kitchen table as someone entered the house.

"Is anyone here?"

She crawled on her hands and knees across the floor to the far end of the table as the intruder came further inside. The legs of the boy stopped directly in front of her, between her and the cellar door.

"You can come out." The boy's voice was kind. "I just want to meet you."

She didn't move for a moment, then she slowly crawled out from under the table and stood facing the boy.

"Hi," said the tall boy with a gentle smile and bright green eyes. "My name is Roger." He was holding a long gray sheet under his arm. "What's your name?"

"I don't remember," she told him.

"I was wondering who you are because I see you out on the back porch all the time."

"You do? Most people can only see ghosts on Halloween."

"You don't look like a ghost," Roger told her. "You seem like a regular girl to me."

He smiled at her, and she averted her eyes.

"What's it like to be..." he began. "You know?"

"It's not bad."

"Aren't you lonely? Don't you miss being with your friends?"

"I never had any friends when I was alive," she said.

"I don't have any friends, either."

"What about those other boys?"

"Oh, that's my older brother Dennis, and his friend Alex. I was trick-or-treating with my cousin Dylan, when those big boys came along and took our candy. Dylan ran home crying and I came here to get our candy back. I thought maybe you could help me."

"*Me*, help you?"

"Sure."

"What do I have to do?" she asked.

"Do you ever scare people?"

"I try not to scare anybody."

"But you could? I mean, if you wanted."

"I guess so," she said. Roger smiled at her, and she couldn't help but smile back. "And you'll be my friend if I help you?"

"We're already friends," Roger told her.

When he finished telling her his plan, the sound of shattering glass caused them to look up.

"Okay," Roger said. "Let's go."

A moment later, they disappeared into the basement as the two teens entered the house through the broken window, shining light from their phones around the living room. The sparse furnishings were festooned with cobwebs and covered in a half inch of dust that rendered everything colorless.

"This place is creepy," Alex declared. "I say we get out of here."

"Let's see what we got first," Dennis said as he opened one of the bags and reached inside.

Alex fixed the light from his phone on Dennis, whose eyes

widened in sudden terror. When he pulled his hand out of the bag it was swarming with cockroaches. He dropped the pillowcase and shook his arm vigorously to dislodge the vile insects, which fell to the floor and scurried under the sofa and into the nearby walls.

Just then, a small figure under a gray bedsheet appeared out of the gloom and stopped near the boys.

Dennis instantly recognized the homemade costume that his younger brother had been wearing. "Roger, what are you doing here?" He reached down and pulled the sheet away. It drifted to the floor, but there was no one there.

"What the –"

Something began to move inside the other pillowcase Dennis was holding and he promptly released it. It struck the floor with a heavy THUD and out rolled a severed head, coming to a stop face up. When Dennis saw his brother looking up at him, he did a doubletake and took a step back. He nearly tripped as he set out quickly in the opposite direction. Alex followed closely behind in a panic as the light from his phone went out and it became as black as a tomb inside the old house.

They searched the endless darkness for a way out until they found the window and jumped through the broken pane of glass without hesitating. Once outside, the boys ran back across the lawn and into the street, never looking back before disappearing into the night.

Watching from the broken window, Roger and the ghost laughed.

"That was awesome!" Roger said. He looked down at the pumpkin lying on the floor and nudged it with his foot. "Did you see the look on my brother's face when he thought it was my head."

"It was nothing," she said.

"Nothing? It was nothing short of spectacular."

She blushed. "Thank you for being my friend." She stepped close to Roger and gave him a hug. Even though she did not have a physical body, he felt her embrace.

# Pets

## *Douglas Goodell*

If any of the residents of Webb Street had been out and about past midnight on Saturday, they would have seen a peculiar sight. But the street was deserted at that late hour. The cool fog was heavy along the street. Two dark figures sauntered out of the fog and stopped by the side of a dim, gaslight streetlamp. A huge grey-black spider was attached by an iron-linked leash to a tall thin girl curiously dressed in a frilly blue dress and white bonnet. The spider was as big as a large dog.

The leash was curled around the spider's front foreleg and connected to a leather collar around the girl's neck. The spider looked both ways before she stepped off the sidewalk gently dragging the blank-looking girl behind. The girl walked mechanically as the leash tugged her along. The spider had four pairs of black eyes, with fur that was trimmed and well groomed. A variety of brightly polished gold and silver jewelry adorned the spider's limbs. A pink beret, stylishly cocked on the spider's head completed the ensemble. The spider's sharp mandibles clicked frequently.

Most spiders were afraid of people and either killed them immediately or ran away screaming from the sight of them. Ariadne was not afraid of people; in fact, she kept this one as a pet. To not frighten her fellow spiders, Ariadne only took her human out on a leash at night. After all, the human deserved some exercise after being cooped up in a glass tank all day long. Ariadne could not leave her pet at home alone in the nest; humans simply could not stay out of trouble; they were curious critters and expert climbers

Ariadne had acquired her human from a Homo Sapien Rescue League facility. The girl was about to be euthanized due to a lack of space at the facility. Ariadne had just fallen in love with the human's long blond hair and clear blue eyes. Ariadne loved to caress the girl with the soft bristles on her limbs. They were so cute at this age! The facility was run by a grossly fat tarantula that had a soft spot in her arachnid heart for the lower animals. Ariadne's human had been lobotomized so she would not run away or try to hurt the spider. She was also spayed because if left unsupervised humans reproduced rapidly. It simply would not be proper to have a bunch of tiny mewling humans running around Ariadne's tidy domicile. The girl was housebroken and quite docile.

The one thing that bothered Ariadne was how fussy her human was about her food. Humans were all notoriously picky eaters. The tarantula had told Ariadne that her human only ate curds and whey which were extremely difficult to find.

Ariadne sighed and looked at her human with affection and just a trace of pity. What we are willing to do for our pets, thought Ariadne. Then they continued on to the Twenty-Four-Hour Pet Food Store.

# God of Thunder

## *Reed Beebe*

The nervous bank teller kept silent as the goon wearing the skull mask pointed a gun at her, commanding her to fill the bag with cash. The robber's similarly masked associates herded customers and the injured security guard to the bank's front entrance to deter any police who might rush the building. All of this occurred under the earnest supervision of the notorious Malefic. The supervillain checked his wristwatch, confirming his crew was on schedule. The city's superhero team—The Adventurers—was diverting an offshore tanker collision that had been arranged by Malefic. Malefic's crew would be gone before the heroes returned to the city.

Ariel Crane kept her eyes down and her hands on her head; she and the other hostages knelt near the bank's large glass doors as directed. Crane had covered Malefic's schemes on multiple occasions, and was calm as she assessed the situation. The award-winning journalist had witnessed Malefic's defeat at the hands of The Adventurers over the years. She hoped that her heroes would come to the rescue, and said a silent prayer that a hero was nearby.

———•———

Home from his shift, flabby hotel night auditor, John Flaubert ate chips on his apartment's sofa as he watched the morning news. Flaubert had anticipated more adventure when he came to the city a few months ago, but he had fallen into a dull routine. He was considering going to bed when he heard someone's prayer.

———•———

Malefic spotted Crane among the hostages. He had considered pulling her from the other captives to gloat about his plan but thought better of it. Despite his current confidence, Malefic knew humility. Beneath his bright-blue skull mask, the villain's face had scars from dozens of capers foiled by The Adventurers. The Athlete had kicked out his two front teeth; the Space Cadet had left a scar on his nose. But this time, the plan was foolproof. The Adventurers would not arrive in time to stop him.

Crane felt the terror among her fellow captives. Some were sobbing. She was making mental notes of the incident. She planned to write an exclusive story for her paper after The Adventurers saved the day, and wanted to remember the sights and sounds around her. Then she noticed the smell.

Malefic heard gasps from the hostages. One of his crew shouted "Who farted?" Malefic saw his henchmen wave their hands in front of their masks to fan away the stench. He felt nauseous when he caught the scent that had caused the distraction in his ranks. He wondered if some of his captives had crapped their pants, then his stomach rumbled. His henchmen laughed after his bottom erupted with a loud fart.

Embarrassed, Malefic shouted at his men, to get them back on task and distract from his shame. The villain heard other eruptions throughout the bank's marble lobby, as his henchmen lost control over their bowels. The cacophony of noisy farts was interrupted by the sound of breaking glass when a tubby man wearing a toga jumped down from the bank's skylight. Malefic feared that The Adventurers had made it back to stop him, but he did not recognize the man that had landed in front of him. Malefic fired his pistol at the stranger.

The fat man was unaffected by Malefic's gunshots. Though he had assumed the guise of lackluster mortal John Flaubert when he came to the city, Crepitus was a god, although not a very celebrated one like his fellow Olympians; a god of flatulence does not inspire worship or temples. Largely forgotten, Crepitus set out to raise his profile among mortals, ignoring Jupiter's edict that the gods leave Earth alone. The humans had a modern pantheon of champions— superheroes—and Crepitus yearned to be one.

"Cease, villains! I am Crepitus, god of Olympus, and these mortals are under my protection!" Crepitus thought even Hercules would be impressed with his entrance.

Noting the hero's invulnerability to bullets, Malefic was unclear whether the stranger was indeed a god, or an out-of-shape super-powered mortal frat boy with delusions of grandeur. Malefic unsheathed a poison-tipped dagger from the scabbard on his belt and lunged at Crepitus.

But then Malefic farted, and so did his henchmen, over and over. Even the distressed hostages started laughing, and Crane laughed the loudest. The distraction was all Crepitus needed; he punched Malefic, breaking the villain's nose.

Malefic fell to the floor, letting out one final fart in his defeat. Malefic's henchmen tried to take Crepitus down with gunfire, but soon realized the futility of their actions, and decided to run. No hostages were hurt, and no money taken.

Later, Crane gave a statement to the police, detailing how the city's new hero had departed the scene, flying through the broken skylight above (she did not mention that he had issued a mighty fart as he did so). Back at her office, Crane's online research confirmed that there was indeed an obscure mythic god of flatulence named "Crepitus" that many scholars considered a literary hoax by ancient Roman satirists. Crane wrote her story and submitted it by the deadline. Alone in her office, she farted, and laughed.

The next morning, Malefic read Crane's article in jail. The villain felt humiliated, and vowed that he would destroy Crepitus someday.

Flaubert also read the article early that morning. He was impressed with Crane's writing style; he thought the reporter had captured his heroic qualities with great accuracy, and hoped that his first adventure would be the beginning of a new and better mythology. Crepitus also hoped that Jupiter would not be offended by Crane's humorous headline: "'God of Thunder' Foils Robbery."

# THE LAUGHING RIVER

## *Duncan Shepard*

I remember the first time the river spoke to me. I was just a child, about four years old, and my mother dipped my toes in the flowing ripples. The water tickled me, and I laughed. I was surprised when the water giggled back at me.

This afternoon was different. I wanted to see the river one last time. I turned off my car's engine and opened the door. I admired the somnolent sea of trees before me. The pit of my stomach filled with a familiar feeling... I was home. As often as I moved around the country, this forest and river always felt like home.

The sun hung low in the sky and the light coming through the trees flickered off the running water. An energy shot through me that I hadn't felt in years. It was as if I was a kid again. An odd sense of shyness came over me as I approached my old friend.

"Don't be frightened, it's good to see you," the river bubbled in a gentle voice.

"I'm glad I could visit."

I sat down on my favorite stone and took my shoes off. The grass felt as if I was stepping into my favorite pair of slippers.

"I'm sorry it's been so long since I visited. Are you ever sad to see so your friends grow old?"

"It does sadden me, but it's the cycle of time. The droplets that make up my flow evaporate into the air and rejoin me after they've fallen from the clouds."

I nodded as the mellow sound of the forest had a soothing effect on my swirling head.

"Your family has always been in tune with nature. I remember one of your grandfathers, hundreds of years ago, exploring the area. That was when I first met your family."

"What was he like?"

"He startled me when he responded to my greeting. Not many people listen close enough to hear me. He was returning home from a bloody war that saw many of his friends killed. We spent hours talking. The battles left scars that others couldn't see. He liked to exist and live in the span of split seconds, which others didn't understand."

"I think I understand that measure of time now. I'm sick and may not see you again, my friend."

"I can sense that you're scared. There's one thing you need to understand... everything is temporary. We might have different lifespans, but we all face the inevitable change from what we once were into something new. One day, I will dry up and the fish, the frogs, and plants will need a new place to live."

I looked to the sky as I dipped my feet into the water, and it tickled my toes.

"We spend so much time building walls to separate us from the reality that our time is finite," I said as I watched the clouds change shape.

"Remember when you brought your daughter to see me?"

"I remember that day as if it were only hours ago. She had an instant rapport with you. I was so proud that she saw the value in connecting with the outside world."

I took a deep breath and held it for a second before exhaling.

"There are so many people who have come and gone throughout history. I'm just a single grain of sand on a vast beach. What kind of impact could I have made with my life?"

"As long as I'm in existence, I'll think about you. In a way, your whole family has taken up residence in my memory," the river offered up.

We both laughed at the idea.

"I haven't laughed in a long time. There have been so many dark days," I said as I stood. "Thank you for that gift... just like the first time we met."

I turned from the river and began the trek back to my car. Visions of my grandmother, mother, father, and daughter flooded my mind. A tear rolled down my cheek and evaporated into the air. *A little part of me might make it back to the river*, I thought as I smiled.

Dedicated to my mother, Doreen

# ON THE RUN

## *Kevin Hopson*

"How's the food, Medusa?" Dwayne asked.

I sat on a stool at the bar, taking a bite of my sandwich as Dwayne approached the counter. He had chocolate-colored skin like me, but his dark hair was cropped, which was a sharp contrast to the dreadlocks I sported.

"It's good," I said. "But you know I come here for the company."

Dwayne stared over my shoulder. "You might be changing your mind about the company."

A portly man soon appeared, taking a seat next to me.

"Hey, Jordan," Dwayne said. "What can I get you?"

Jordan eyed my drink. "Whatever the young lady is having. A Bloody Mary, is it?"

"More like cranberry juice," I replied.

A soft chuckle escaped his lips. "Alright. One cranberry juice then."

"This is the woman I told you about," Dwayne said, pouring a glass of cranberry juice and resting it in front of Jordan.

Jordan turned to me, his eyes going wide. "You're Medusa?"

I huffed. "Really, Dwayne? Now you're telling complete strangers about me?"

Dwayne shrugged and flashed his pearly whites.

"Ask me something," Jordan said.

"I just want to eat my lunch in peace."

"One question," he insisted.

I let out a frustrated breath. "Fine." I took a moment to ponder. "Do you have a girlfriend?"

"A handsome guy like me," Jordan snickered. "Of course, I have a girlfriend."

I watched as Jordan's body stiffened. His mouth hung agape, and his brown eyes were completely still.

It was a power of mine. If I asked someone a question and they didn't answer truthfully, they would go into a state of suspended animation. And the spell could only be broken by my touch.

"Maybe I should leave him like this for a while," I said to Dwayne.

Dwayne couldn't stifle a laugh. "It makes no difference to me. But if he can't pay, I'm charging you for the cranberry juice," he said with a wink.

I placed a hand on Jordan's shoulder, and he immediately gasped.

"Wow," Jordan said, his eyes bulging. "That was intense. And kind of scary, if I'm being honest."

"That's the point," I said.

My phone buzzed. I pulled it from the front pocket of my

jeans and answered the call.

"Hey, Carl," I said.

"Hey, Medusa. Is this a bad time?"

"No. What's up?"

"I need your help with something. Are you free?"

"I have some time," I said.

"Great. Where are you at?"

"The Olive Grove Grill."

"Can I swing by and pick you up? I'll drop you back at your car later."

"Sure."

———

Braxton Miles," Carl said from the driver's seat of his car. "He was arrested on one count of grand theft auto. It's a low-level felony, but it can still carry up to three years in prison. Anyway, he didn't appear at his court hearing this morning."

I glanced at Carl from the passenger seat. He was a stocky guy with a perpetual five o'clock shadow. Carl was a fugitive recovery agent, or what most people referred to as a bounty hunter. He worked for a local bail bondsman, and he'd been trying to lure me into the profession for months. But I was happy with my private investigation business.

"So, where are we headed?" I asked.

"Braxton's girlfriend's house."

I arched an eyebrow. "Really?"

Carl nodded. "It's always the first place I look. You'd be surprised how many times I've found bail skippers at their girlfriend's house."

"It seems too obvious."

"That's the thing. Most of these guys are idiots. If they were smart, they never would have gotten caught in the first place."

"How do you know about the girlfriend?"

Carl couldn't help but smile. "Facebook. It's another gold mine for information. A lot of these guys haven't got a clue what privacy settings are. They just post everything publicly."

A couple of minutes later, Carl pulled to the side of the road and parked behind another sedan.

"Just give me a minute," he said.

He exited the car, briefly conversed with the driver in front of us, then eased behind the wheel again.

"Who was that?" I said.

"Another buddy I occasionally work with. The girlfriend's house is down the street. He already checked, and no one appears to be home. There's no car in the driveway and no activity inside the house. But he's going to stay and case the place."

"What are we going to do?"

Carl pondered. "Where's the closest gas station?"

My brow furrowed. "I think the Valero station at the corner of Bailey Drive and Dola Mine Road. Why?"

"Braxton is a smoker. I used to be one as well. With the anxiety he's likely feeling right now, he'll be craving a smoke. Or ten," he joked.

"Let me guess," I said. "Facebook."

Carl chuckled. "You got it. But even if it wasn't common knowledge, I'd still bet on it. Eighty percent of bail skippers I've caught are smokers."

"You're kidding?"

Carl shook his head. "Nope. In fact, I've apprehended several guys at gas stations. Even if Braxton isn't there, it's worth checking out."

———◆———

The door dinged as we stepped inside the gas station convenience store. Carl walked toward the counter, and I sidled up to him. A lanky teenage boy sat behind the counter, fiddling with something in his lap.

I noticed Carl glimpse his phone.

"What is it?" I muttered.

"The girlfriend just returned," he replied. "But she was alone."

I inspected the store, spotting a couple of security cameras.

"Why would he risk coming here if they have security cameras?" I said.

Carl raised an eyebrow as if saying, "Why do you think?"

"Right," I whispered. "Stupidity."

Carl bobbed his head in agreement.

"Can I help you with something?" the teenager asked, getting to his feet.

"Yeah," Carl said, holding his phone up to the boy. "Have you seen this man?"

I noticed the boy's eyes widen ever so slightly.

"No," he said, shaking his head.

"I think he's lying," I said.

"I'm not lying," the boy shouted. "I haven't seen him."

Carl looked at me. "You should ask him yourself."

I met the boy's gaze. "Have you seen the man in the photo?"

"I just told you. I haven't seen him."

My spell took hold, and the boy froze in place.

"You were right," Carl said. "Now what?"

"We make him sweat for a minute."

Carl perused the candy display next to us.

"Okay," I finally said. "Let's free him."

I bent over the counter and touched the boy's shoulder with my index finger.

"What the hell was that?" he said, panting heavily.

"That's what you get when you lie," Carl replied. "Do you want to experience that again?"

The boy shook his head violently.

"Good," Carl said. "Then answer the woman's questions. Truthfully."

"When did he come in?" I asked.

"About fifteen minutes ago," the boy answered, his breathing still labored. "He bought a pack of cigarettes and gave me some cash to keep quiet. In case anyone came looking for him."

"And where is he now?"

"I don't know. He said he had to use the restroom around back, but he could be gone by now."

I turned to Carl.

"I'll call my contact at the police department," he said, already making his way toward the door.

Carl pushed through the door, and I quickly followed on his heels. He stopped along the sidewalk, taking a moment to complete his call. Then Carl pocketed his phone, the two of us walking side by side. As we turned the corner, a man exited one of the restrooms.

"That's him," Carl whispered, snatching the handcuffs from the back of his belt but keeping them hidden.

"I've got this," I muttered.

Braxton glanced up as he approached.

"Hi," I said. "How are you?"

Braxton dipped his head and pursed his lips, completely snubbing me. He passed us, and Carl pivoted in Braxton's direction, ready to spring into action.

I raised a hand to Carl. "Just hold up," I whispered. Then I turned to Braxton. "Hey!"

Braxton stopped and spun around. "What?" he said, clearly agitated.

"Are you okay?"

Braxton's brows scrunched together, and he glared at me as if I was a crazy woman. And maybe I was.

"I'm fine," he said. "Now leave me—"

But Braxton couldn't finish his sentence thanks to my spell.

Carl appeared at my side. "How'd you know that would work?"

"It's a common question, and most people lie when answering. People are rarely fine or okay, especially if they're a fugitive on the run."

Carl smiled. He pulled Braxton's hands behind his back and snapped the handcuffs around Braxton's wrists.

"I'll keep him in suspended animation until the cops get here," I said.

"Are you sure you don't want to join my team?"

"Girlfriends' houses, gas stations, Facebook, and stupid fugitives. Is that your recipe for success?"

Carl chuckled. "Pretty much."

I nodded. "I'll think about it."

# Happy Anniversary

## *James Austin McCormick*

Adam Gentik peered through the plasti-steel glass at the hellish, volcanic landscape outside. His ageing, equine face creased with disapproval.

"Foolish idea," he grumbled. "Positively juvenile. Why endanger oneself for no reason?"

Atikar, the personal representative at Enchanted Travel gave a polished smile. "Mr Gentik, I assure you, our patented magic is the best there is. The Guild of Wizards themselves created the spell we use." He gestured to the cowled figure beside him.

The man bowed.

"And our most highly qualified charm caster is here to transform you into lava angels personally. You'll find this dimension quite safe, and I dare say most exhilarating as well." He waved a hand over the sulphurous landscape beyond. "The fire realm is beautiful, is she not? Think of the adventures you and your good lady can have out there. Mrs Gentik has put a great deal of thought into this."

Mrs Gentik, pretty, blond, and at thirty-three, more than half the age of her prudish husband, hooked an arm through his. "That's what I've been telling him, Mr Atikar. Adam's such a boring old stick in the mud but he can't back out this time. I insisted I choose how to celebrate our first wedding anniversary and he agreed." She gave a shrug. "I chose this."

The old man sniffed. "I had no idea you would pick something so ridiculous." His nose wrinkled in disgust. "Magic indeed."

His wife smiled and put her head playfully on her husband's shoulder. "Just humor me this once," she purred, "after that, if you still want me to be the serious, strait-laced wife, then I will be."

Gentik seemed somewhat mollified. "And those frightful parties I demanded you cease attending?"

"After this I'll never go to another one," his wife promised. "If you tell me not to."

His beak nose wrinkled. "And those ghastly friends?"

"All done with."

The old man nodded. "Very well, Susan. It seems you're finally learning your place."

"Oh, but I am," she answered sweetly.

Gentik gave a soft grunt. "Perhaps you won't be the disappointment I feared. Very well. On this single occasion, I will indulge you."

———◆———

"Keep up." The words weren't spoken, but rather conveyed through a series of psychedelic colour changes along the slim, segmented body and the graceful movements of the huge crystalline wings. Susan soared upwards, daring him to climb higher in the dense, furnace-like atmosphere.

He beat his own wings to come up alongside of his wife. She turned; her husband's insect eyes were so dark and huge she could see her own reflection in them. While her form was mostly reds and yellows—usual for the female—his were darker, a mixture of purple and greens. As the male of the species, he was also smaller and weaker than she was.

"Adam," she said, indicating an area ahead with one of her many sets of arms. "That volcanic ridge. Let's go." She sped away, leaving her companion to grumble as he tried to match her superior speed. When he did catch her up at the ridge, he found her riding the thermal currents around the volcano. He hesitated. If he could have swallowed at that moment, he would have.

"Relax," his wife told him. "This is magic. Nothing in this landscape can hurt us."

Her husband's small, cylindrical head tilted to one side, hypnotised by the display. His body quivered with an instinctive excitement and eagerness that was impossible to fight. He dived down to join her.

"Isn't this romantic?" Susan said, pressing herself close to him. "You know, this is how fire angels mate."

"Don't be so ridiculous," her husband scolded her. "Do behave." Yet the heat was intoxicating. Without realising what he was doing, he turned, interlocking his wings with those of his wife. Spines extended from the tips, piercing hers.

They shuddered in unison, bodies erupting in a multi-coloured display of ecstasy. They circled the fiery lake below, following the air currents. With each pass their physical tensions mounted, until at last the inevitable climax released them from their madness.

Immediately, all strength seemed to leave Adam's body. He was too weak to even move his wings.

"Something's wrong," he said.

Susan grabbed him with one of her many arms. "Nothing's wrong, Adam," she told him. "This is how it's supposed to be." She sped upwards, high into the sulphuric clouds.

Her body began to swell. Her limbs became thicker, whilst her mandibles grew to more than double their former size.

"Enough," her husband ordered. "Take me back now."

"Not yet," Susan told him. "We're not finished. You see ..." her jaws snapped, "when a female lava angel mates, she needs nutrients almost immediately, lest the younglings die in her womb. Do you know how she gets them? Take a guess."

He wanted to struggle, but he was too weak to move.

"Her mate offers himself up to her. She eats him."

She saw his terror. If he had a mouth, he would have screamed at that moment.

"Happy anniversary, darling." She made it quick, ripping his head off before she began to devour the body.

———————

"I trust you were satisfied with our service, Mrs Gentik?" Atikar asked, hands folded neatly in front of him.

The woman, dressed in a robe and reclining in a lounger by the pool, nodded. She took a sip of her freshly squeezed orange juice. "I'm so glad I went with the gold magic membership. That extra little 'perk' was really worth having."

"I am so pleased, Mrs Gentik."

"Call me Susan," the woman said. "Now that I'm single again, I'd prefer to just go by my first name."

"But of course."

"Oh dear." Susan laid her drink down, placing a hand to her stomach. For a moment she seemed to be in discomfort.

"Are you alright?" Atikar asked, stepping forward. "On very rare occasions the reversal spell can cause some minor nausea for a short period. Should I send for the charm caster?"

The woman shook her head. "No, I'm fine. Just a touch of indigestion, I think." She flashed the man a smile. "It must be something I ate."

# TRUSTWORTHY

## *Joe Stout*

Sienna woke feeling her book slipping through her fingers. She grabbed at where it should have been falling, but felt nothing.

"What? Hey!"

It disappeared behind a tree almost as soon as she saw it, a flash of bright red skin. Sienna scrambled to her feet and took off after it.

The imp was fast, but Sienna had been raised in the forest and knew every tree and stone. So when the imp tried to cut through a tunnel under a boulder, she was waiting on the other side.

"Ow! You're hurting me!" It cried, dangling by its ears.

"Where's my book?"

"What book? I don't know anything about a book!"

She flipped the beast so it dangled by its feet and shook it. Lots of things fell out from the folds in its skin: coins, watches, keys, a lyre, a live chicken, a pair of shearing scissors, and finally her book. Dropping the imp, she picked it up and brushed off the dirt.

"You didn't have to do all that." The imp rubbed its head. "I just wanted to read it."

"Sure, and what about all that other stuff?"

"Humans don't notice me, so I take things to get their attention. But they never notice, or if they do, they think they're the ones that lost it."

"So why don't you return it?"

The imp sighed. "You don't get it, do you? If I turn up with the missing item, they assume I took it in the first place and get mad about it."

"But you did take it!"

"Expecting them to notice immediately! But they're too distracted to realize until it's too late for me. I'm just playful, but no one wants to see that."

She sighed. "I guess being playful is okay. But not with my books! They're special!"

"What's so special about them?" It rolled its eyes. "Ink on paper. Easy to replace if something happens."

She held the book to her chest. "Not these. These were my mom's."

There was something in the way she said it that told the imp not to joke. "Your mom isn't here anymore."

Sienna shook her head. "No. She died two years ago. Sometimes I think if I read her books, she might still be with me, or whatever part of her that loved these stories is."

"I'm sorry."

"And then you go and take it, and it was like losing her again. I didn't know what to do."

"I was going to bring it back, honest! You were sleeping, and I figured I'd be done with it by the time you woke up."

She stopped for a second. "Can imps read?"

"Of course we can! We can read, write, do sums, even the occasional bit of algebra."

"What's algebra?"

"It's like math, but worse. We use it to make sure our tricks won't harm anyone."

"But why do you do tricks?"

It shrugged. "We're just trying to be friendly. We don't have a lot of friends."

"Oh." She looked down at the book in her hands, then up at the imp. "What's your name?"

"Beezlebak."

"Beezlebak?" She scrunched her nose. "That's a weird name."

"What's yours?"

"Sienna."

It nodded. "That's just as weird as Beezlebak."

"At least you can say it!"

The imp laughed. "If you'll be my friend, you can call me Beez."

She thought for a moment. "Okay, Beez." Sienna held out the book. "You can borrow this if you want."

"Really?"

She nodded. "I've already finished it twice. Just be really careful with it."

———◆———

Sienna spent the night tossing and turning. She never should have given her book to that imp. Everyone knew imps were untrustworthy, and while it wasn't her favorite of her mother's books, it was still important to her.

"You look tired," her father said when she came in for breakfast.

"Couldn't sleep." She took a ladle and scooped herself a bowl of porridge.

"That's not good."

She sighed as she sat down. "I think I trusted something I shouldn't have."

"What makes you say that?" He folded his newspaper and sat it on the table.

"Something wanted to borrow one of my books, and they were so pitiful, I let them, and now I'm scared I'll never get it back."

"Something?"

"An imp."

He nodded. "I was friends with an imp when I was your age."

"You were?"

"It was trustworthy. One of the more trustworthy friends I've ever had. Everyone else looked down on it, but all it wanted was a friend. It gave back to me everything I gave it and more. Respect, kindness, even some silliness."

"Are you still friends with it?"

He shook his head. "No, something happens when you grow up. I loved ol' Beez, but I lost the things we had in common, and we drifted apart."

Sienna smiled. "Beez? That was its name?"

"Yeah. Smart little guy, loyal as hell. Sometimes I wonder what happened to him."

She smiled. "I bet he's doing okay."

"I hope so. Anyway, I hope your imp is as trustworthy as Beez was."

"I'm feeling better about it, Dad."

The next day, Sienna was sleeping under a different tree when she woke to the feeling of her book slipping from her hands. She looked up and saw Beez smiling at her. "I finished the other one."

Sienna laughed. The other book was sitting on the ground.

"Come on, Beez. Let's go to my house. You can pick out some books to borrow."

"Really?"

"Yeah. And I know a guy that'd like to see you."

"Who's that?"

"It's a surprise," she smiled.

Beez laughed and took her hand, and together they walked through the forest.

# IN THE NIGHT GARDEN

## *Bethany Pope*

Things have gotten stranger in the garden. It was nothing much at first, nothing too noticeable. The flowers on the cucumber vines developed an odd color—the morbid purple shade of a fresh, deep bruise, swallowing the yellow. Then the frilled leaves of the carrots began to fuse, the fronds developing an odd, skin-like texture. The peanut plants were next: the leaves and stalks began to thicken, until the shapes of the plants began to resemble large, fleshy hands, thrusting their way clear of the soil, as though they were trying to call down the sky.

They still looked like plants, don't get me wrong. They were becoming fun-house mirror versions of themselves, but the transformation wasn't so dramatic that anyone but a careful gardener would notice. If you saw the garden in passing, perhaps from the road or riding by on a bicycle, you might not cotton onto the fact that anything was off kilter at all. But I've been working on this land for years (since well before the kids moved away; back before Bea died, when we worked it together) and I could note the difference at once.

Bea would have seen it, too. Hell, she would probably have seen it before I did. She always had her head screwed on right, my Bea. And it's likely that she'd know how to handle it. Better than I do, at any rate.

'Hattie,' she'd say, in that laughing way she had, when I was being stupid and she was loving me, despite it, 'remember those old Hidden Pictures puzzles the children liked? This is a similar situation. You can't win by focusing on all those little details. You have to take the whole image in at once and look for the odd shapes. Wait for the Hidden Images to pop out at you. Then, all of a sudden, you'll see it all at once and wonder how you missed something so obvious.'

I can hear her voice so clearly in my head. It's as though she were standing right here, next to me, resting her soft brown hair on my shoulder and running her long fingers over the back of my neck.

So that's what I've been trying to do. It's madness of course, taking advice from the dead. It's even worse when you know for a fact that her voice is really nothing more than your own interior narrative; all gussied up, wearing a mask based on your wife's dear face.

At any rate, madness or not, this was the only advice that I had to hand. I couldn't exactly call the cops. Can you imagine the conversation?

'Hello? 911? I'd Like to report a crime. What crime, you ask? Oh, someone is transforming my vegetables into human skin. Why yes, officer, I'll be happy to sit right here until you send the paramedics. Thanks so much for your help.'

I can't call the children either. Tommy has only been

living in his dorm for three weeks. I don't want to interrupt his studies. And Judy just began her internship. It's a huge opportunity for her, and she loves me so much that she'd throw it all away and be on the next flight back to Lemon Orchards five minutes after we said our goodbyes.

No, this is one problem that I have to untangle all by myself; with no help, save for Bea's echoes inside of my head.

So that's what I've been doing; trying to see the shapes buried in the big picture, the ones that my detail-oriented brain doesn't want to consider. I'll spend the early morning completing all the usual chores: pulling up weeds, watering, deadheading the oddly lip-like roses, pulling up the odd, organ-like stragglers (even the ones that seem to bleed when the roots are cut), adding fertilizer wherever the strange vegetation seems to need it.

For a while, I thought that the pumpkins were dying. They were all turning brown, their rinds becoming pliant—bouncy and rubbery as the skin on a plump stomach. I'd poke a finger in, and it would sink, as though into a loose covering of fat, but the surface tension never broke, and the rind would bounce back afterwards. It was like poking a belly, or a breast.

I kept drenching them in water and fertilizer, hoping that I'd instigate a change, and they just kept growing. They swelled up, bigger and bigger, their color deepening to a rich, honey brown. I was worried that they were going to split, disgorging God only knows what all over the grass. But then, after a few days, I woke up in the middle of the night, shocked out of bed with the realization that the pumpkins had shifted into the exact same shade as Bea's skin.

When I examined one closely, crouched in the dark with

a torch in my hands, I discovered that they each bore a mark that looked, unmistakably, like the mole that was to the left of Bea's sweet cup of a navel. It was like a little black star. I used to run my fingers over it when we were making love. I called it my lucky star. It looked so harmless. Until it started to grow.

How were we to know that it was melanoma?

I was weeping then, in the night-drenched garden, stroking that stupid pumpkin as the tears flowed and flowed and the morning lightened into day.

And that's when I saw the Hidden Picture. I saw it as the sun climbed, clear as the sunlight I was sitting in.

Bea loved this garden as much, or more, than I did. She loved it in much the same way that she loved me, or our children. She poured so much of her heart into the soil over the years. Now, that the long drought had come, the garden had decided that it was time to give a little of it back.

I was laughing then. A mad, unhinged sound. I could hear the madness even as the torrential laughter tore its way out through my throat and into the sky.

I didn't care. All madness has a shard of truth buried in it. That truth is love.

My wife is dead and in the soil. But she loved the soil. And now the garden is growing a new fruit.

There's one pumpkin in particular that looks as though it'll be ripened any day now. I can't even rightly call it a pumpkin anymore, not with the way the gourd has lengthened. It's as though it's been divided into three pieces—head, middle, legs—with those four, long splits on the sides and at the bottom. There are five blunt vines curling out of the ends of the each of the arms, and they have started occasionally twitching.

There is nothing there that looks like her dark hair, but it's early yet. I can wait. And of course, there are those slow, soft beginnings of her sweet face.

All I have to do is wait, care for it, and be ready for the harvest when it comes at last. And when this fruit is ripe, once the vine leading down into her brain is severed, I know that she'll open those dark, clear eyes of hers. I know that she'll look at me, and smile. Perhaps she'll speak.

I know that when this body begins, as all fruit must, to sag and rot as her first body did, that there will be another pumpkin ready there, to replace it. Or a tomato. Or an eggplant. Each in its season.

As I said before. I'm patient. I can wait.

# Love Filter

## *Gregg Chamberlain*

Old Mob lived alone, except for her aged cat, Corif, in a shanty near the desert's edge. The nearest village was a morning's walk or a day's hobble away. Mob sometimes went there to trade what she had for what she wanted.

Daily she and Corif followed the caravan trails. He hobbled about his business in the sand while she poked the sands with her stick, looking for stuff fallen along the trail that she could use or sell.

One day Corif uncovered a wine amphora with the seal still intact. Mob looked the jug over carefully, thinking of the silver it would bring at the village inn. *I could stand a little wine myself,* she thought. *Should check the contents anyway.*

The seal was old clay and broke easily. She looked inside. Empty. She held the amphora upside-down. Nothing.

Nothing inside except air that was so old and stale it was green. It poured out of the jug. And out, and out, forming a little green cloud above Mob's head. And in the cloud was a face.

"Blessings on you, oh ancient crone, for freeing me from my prison. Name your reward and I shall grant whatever you wish, if it lies within my power to do so."

Old Mob licked her gums. "What I want is to be young and beautiful again and know the love of a handsome, lusty young man. Make me again the woman I was at eighteen and make my cat," she said, pointing at a shivering Corif, "a strong, handsome young man."

"Done! Come tomorrow's dawning you shall have your wish." The cloud thinned and was gone.

Mob clapped her wrinkled hands and, muttering excitedly to herself, hobbled home where she cooked a hasty supper and then tucked herself and her cat in bed.

In the morning when Mob awoke, she immediately remembered the jinn's words. She felt no aches or pains such as had plagued her lately in the morning. Tentatively her hands explored beneath the thin blanket. And found round, firm breasts thrusting up against the coarse wool, a flat, smooth belly untouched by childbirth, and soft, sleek thighs unmarked by ugly blue veins.

Then she thought of Corif. She turned and saw a godling lying on his side next to her. Head propped on his right hand, he looked into her eyes and smiled.

Oh, goddess of love, Mob thought. A warrior, a titan, a Man! Smiling, she reached out and pulled him to her.

Corif grinned and sang in a sweet soprano, "Aren't you sorry now you took me to the village surgeon for that little operation?"

# A Visit to the Dragon

## *Andrew Kurtz*

The wizard approached the princess while she was preparing for bed.

"I apologize for disturbing your highness, but the dragon requires an audience with you in his cave tonight," the wizard informed her.

"If this is a joke, you will be executed right now. Why should a smelly unintelligent beast who lives in a cave surrounded by mountains of treasure, want to see me?" the princess questioned, opening her mouth wide to yawn.

"The dragon has protected our kingdom for hundreds of years against any enemies who would harm us. Without his aid, we might be slaves to an army of goblins or dinner for hungry trolls. You used to be kind and loving, now you are cruel. The people are starving, while you and your friends have feasts every night with enough food that would feed our kingdom. Yet you give your loyal subjects the bare minimum to eat. The elderly and sick are dying of starvation. You execute people who have committed no crimes, just so you can be entertained. I am not asking you to visit the dragon, I am insisting," the wizard stated as ten of the princess' guards approached with swords pointed directly at her.

"I get the point. After I meet with this foul creature, I am going to execute all of you for treason," the princess threatened, putting on her dress which contained numerous pockets.

The dragon's cave was musty, yet the numerous piles of treasure distracted the princess from the nauseating odor.

The dragon was thirty feet long, covered in green scales, had two ten-foot wings, a long neck, and a tail that was covered in sharp spikes at the end.

"I have better things to do than visit a reptile at night," the princess remarked, attempting to stuff as much treasure into her pockets as possible.

"A thief as well," the dragon stated, releasing a stream of flame near the princess, causing her to leap back.

"I deserve this more than you. I would spend it on enhanced execution devices, to kill more people in less time. Think of all the food I can buy with this from the other kingdoms, not for the people, but me," she explained.

"A dragon's lifespan is more than thousand years and during that time we gain a great deal of knowledge. One of the things I have recently discovered is that you aren't the real princess, but an imposter intent on destroying the kingdom. Tell me where the princess is hidden, and I will let you live. If you refuse, I will reduce you to ashes," the dragon warned.

"I am the real princess, you dumb oaf!" the princess yelled.

The dragon laughed as smoke arose from its nostrils.

"Last chance. Reveal the location, or take it to your grave," the dragon threatened.

The princess began to convulse as though having an epileptic seizure. In the end, the princess was gone and in her place was a gray humanoid figure devoid of any facial or body characteristics.

"We are superior to all of humanity and should be its rulers. I can shape-shift into any form I desire. I can transform as small as a mouse or as large as a dragon. The real princess is in her castle, deep in the dungeons. She has been fed bread and water daily, she is chained to a wall, has a rancorous body odor and shreds of clothing," the shapeshifter explained.

"Well done. I will verify this fiend's story immediately," the wizard said and vanished into the air.

A few moments later, he reappeared with a woman who looked more like a beggar than a princess. Her hair was full of lice, her skin filthy, and her clothes practically non-existent.

"Why have you allowed the Princess to live and not executed her as you do to the people?" the wizard asked.

"I enjoyed seeing her in this depraved condition. A royal princess reduced to a mere beggar is glorious," the shapeshifter boasted.

"You monster!" cried the wizard, as he raised his wand to release a spell, but remained by a look from the dragon.

"I have held my part of the bargain and returned the infidel. Now release me you overgrown toad" the shapeshifter demanded.

"Yes, you can go," the dragon said, glancing at the woman who was the rightful princess.

As the shapeshifter began to leave, the dragon let loose a burst of flame that disintegrated the creature instantly.

"You may go to Hell," the dragon snarled,

After a few days, the princess was returned to her rightful state. Each family was given an abundance of food and executions were a thing of the past.

# BIKER WITCH

## *Kyla Chapek*

What kind of bar opened at 7 a.m.? Unfortunately, the bar I used to work at in my late twenties. When I was the rookie bartender on staff at the Mom and Pop's diner/sports bar off of highway 99N, I was given all the opening early morning shifts. Since I had to count all the money out for the till on top of the other opening tasks, I had to arrive earlier than anyone else as well.

Despite the ungodly hour, we still had customers in the bar right when I opened the door. One morning a handful of leather-clad bikers were waiting for me when I unlocked the door. They went straight for the lottery machines that lined one full wall of the bar.

One biker couple fed a twenty into the jukebox and boogied down on the dancefloor like New Year's had come early. They giggled and smooched under the mistletoe that decorated the bar in honor of the Christmas season. I had served the couple before and knew them as Riff and Darla. The middle-aged couple rode with the Free Souls Motorcycle Club.

The greying-haired leather-clad pair dirty danced like horny teenagers for a long time, but after a few Bloody Mary drinks the mood changed. Darla freaked out on Riff. She shouted a slurry of profanities that would make a sailor blush, slapped him across the face and marched outside to the smoking area.

I just shook my head at the display. It was not the first time the two had gotten into a public argument. Riff went outside after Darla and twenty minutes later they returned laughing and hanging all over each other. Riff came up to the bar laughing about how he needed to keep his Biker Witch happy or she would put a curse on him. I just shook my head. As long as they paid their bill and didn't bother the other customers they could fight and make up all they wanted.

———————

A week later I clocked in at 6:20 a.m. "Another day, another dollar," I sighed as I started the coffee.

When I walked through the swinging double doors leading to the bar, I was startled by the sudden tune of *Santa Claus is Coming to Town*. With an irritated growl I turned to remove the batteries from the singing moose head on the wall that was part of the Christmas decorations. I hated the damn thing and didn't know who kept putting the batteries back in. When the lyrics of the song registered in my tired brain my hand froze in the air.

"Shyla, Shyla is coming to town. Shyla sees you when you're sleeping, Shyla knows when you're awake..." The moose's head, adorned with a Santa hat, bobbed back and forth as it sang.

"What the hell?" I said out loud as the moose continued to add my name to the lyrics over and over again.

The accompanying music changed to the tune of *Jingle Bells*, but the sing-song voice had very different lyrics.

"Do not turns, me me offs, I am not a moooose...it is Riffff stuck in here, get me out out of here please. Hey!"

With mouth agape, I blinked my eyes and shook my head. I had officially not gotten enough sleep. Was I hallucinating?

"Please, Shyla, that damn witch made me like this. I need your help. It took me forever to be able to sing anything but the Christmas songs." The voice was still sing songy but didn't follow a tune I recognized.

"Wha, what do you want me to do?" I felt stupid and couldn't believe I asked the question.

"Darla says I won't turn back until I get one of the girls to dance for me while I sing. It's the only thing that will break the curse. Please, Shyla, I can't stand these Christmas songs anymore. They're driving me insane."

I could relate to that. "So, what, all I got to do is dance and you'll turn back?"

"Yes! I just need you to dance. Hurry before anyone else gets here!"

The tune from *Jingle Bell Rock* spewed from the moose's mouth.

"Okay," I said dubiously. Still half convinced I was asleep in bed and having a very realistic dream, I swayed back and forth and snapped my fingers to the beat. What could it hurt?

"You have to get into it or it won't work," said the moose between verses.

I rolled my eyes. "Fine!" Loosening up I over-exaggerated

shaking my hips to the beat. After a verse I got into it and delved deep into my limited stock pile of dance moves. As the song ended, I did a fancy spin move and ended with my back to the moose head.

The music stopped and my ears popped. I stood straight and turned. I nearly screamed when I found Riff standing behind me, wearing nothing but a Santa hat on his head . The middle-aged man blushed and covered his naughty parts with the Santa hat.

"I um, I'll just be going, I um, thanks kid."

I watched opened-mouthed as the bare-assed biker made a hasty retreat out the side door of the restaurant. Not sure if I had really seen what I had just seen, I continued on with my opening routine. What else could I do? The next time the biker couple came in, Riff made no reference to the singing moose incident, but from then on, he always gave me an extra big tip.

# Cats, Rats, Bats, and Automobiles

## John A. Frochio

Wendy Wilhelm left her home and coven as soon as she was able. To her mother's dismay, she never acted like a normal witch. She loved shopping at unique stores in exotic locations. Wendy abandoned her bewitching habits in favor of more worldly pleasures.

Her sisters Wanda and Wilma berated her regularly with voice and text messages, email tirades, twitter squawks, and not-so-subtle Facebook postings. Wendy attributed their nastiness to jealousy of her good looks and worldly freedoms. Wendy's drop-dead gorgeous attributes included long black hair, slim legs, an hourglass figure, and sultry pouting lips. She had become, in fact, an almost famous supermodel.

One day, after a long spell (not *that* kind of spell) without work, Wendy was sunning herself on a Nassau beach when her cell phone blared. Since that usually meant work, she hastily answered it without checking the caller ID. To her surprise, the caller was her sister Wanda. She groaned. She almost never got phone calls from family anymore.

"What's up, Wanda?"

"Don't throw your worldly spells at me, sister. I'm immune to temptations of the flesh."

"Sitting alone at the old homestead, eh, Wanda?"

"Shut up and listen. We need all the family back here right away. The family business is going under, and we need a powerful spell from the entire witches' coven to save it."

Wendy sighed. "Are you serious?"

"Dead serious. We need to invoke the Strong Sister Spell from the great circle of witches that resists the powerful forces of capitalism and politics."

Well, she couldn't argue with that. The Strong Sister Spell was one of the most powerful spells you can invoke. Maybe she could slip in an extra chant for more modeling gigs.

"Okay. I'll get there as fast as you can."

Using her iPhone, Wendy tried booking a flight for the next morning. Insufficient funds! She tried credit. Maxed out!

What a fine cauldron of fish!

However, she wasn't surprised. She'd been living life a little too large, and lately she was being bypassed for younger models. She wondered briefly if her sisters had anything to do with that, casting long distance spells of retribution. No, they wouldn't waste their time or energy.

She checked out of her room and called a driverless uber. Fortunately, she had some cash. She directed the autopilot to take her to the nearest port. When she arrived, she tried to book a cabin on a ship, to no avail. While she pondered other options, a boy in rags appeared out of nowhere, snatched her purse and disappeared into the aether.

"Hey! Get back here!"

Grumbling, she followed his ionic dust trail to an old, battered fishing boat. She sensed he was inside the vessel.

She said, "I know you're in there. Come out and I won't call the cops."

A grizzled old man with a pointy nose and ratlike whiskers hobbled over to Wendy on a shaky peg leg. He took off his sailor's cap and said, "May I be of service, ma'am?"

He bowed, toppling to the dock.

She helped him up.

"Aren't you an almost famous supermodel or something?"

"Yeah, something. Anyway, I need to get back to the states, to Pennsylvania, as soon as possible. Can you help?"

"Why don't you fly?"

"Well, my broom... I mean, I'm afraid of flying." Actually, she was afraid of brooms. An aversion to cleaning. "So, you know, just boats, trains, automobiles, and the occasional land animal."

"It'll take a while, but I can get you to Florida."

"Close enough! Also, the boy hiding in your boat stole my purse."

He shrugged and almost tipped over. "Don't know anything about that. So, no money?"

"I'm good for it. Rich and almost famous, you know."

He looked her up and down. "Okay. I'm Cap'n Amos Ratatouille."

He reached out a hand and hit the deck again.

84

The next morning as the sun peeked over the horizon, they set sail. After several hours of calm waters, the sea became choppier, the wind grew stronger, and the sky grew darker.

———————

Casually stretched out on a lounger in a red string bikini, Wendy yawned. "Storm coming?"

Before Cap'n Amos could respond, a giant tsunami rose up from the sea like an enraged sea monster. Wendy screamed. The old sailor screamed. A tiny voice down below screamed. Wendy shouted, "Hey, it's the kid." Cap'n Amos yelled, "Sorry. My son. Always getting into trouble." He chuckled weakly.

Then it hit them.

The next thing she knew, she was lying on a rocky shore, battered and hurting all over. She staggered to her feet. If only she had her phone GPS.

A few yards away, the soaking wet Cap'n was stumbling about like a drunken sailor. Before Wendy's astounded eyes, he morphed into a rat and scurried off, hastily followed by a smaller rat. They disappeared into thick woods. Since she was used to far stranger things in the modeling industry, she shook it off and started walking.

As she wandered aimlessly, in pain with each step, she remembered what her mother had once told her about the Strong Sister Spell. *Use it sparingly,* she said, *for it's too powerful to use lightly. If you don't respect its power, it could reverse your spell three times worse than what you desire.* She trembled at her words.

Eventually she found herself in an abandoned industrial park. The sun began to set.

She heard a soft mew. A cat peeked around a building,

padded over to her, and rubbed on her legs. Cats always liked her. She wondered if they'd be willing to help her.

She caterwauled. Soon she was surrounded by thirteen cats.

*Excellent. The perfect number. For a witch anyway.*

She spoke cat. "I need your help. Go find all the yarn you can and bring it to me."

Soon they returned batting balls of yarn all over the place. Under her bewitching direction, they gradually constructed a human-sized rug.

"Now take me to where bats hang out."

The cats led her to a windowless, deteriorated building. The sun had set, and a full moon lit the parking lot. She called out to the bats. In short order, thirteen bats fluttered around her.

Perfect. Exactly thirteen were required for the spell to work. No more, no less.

"I need a ride through the night."

She stretched out on the rug, securing herself with strands of yarn, and commanded the bats to lift her into the sky.

"To Pittsburgh, Pennsylvania," she commanded, bespelling the bats with super speed.

She bid the cats goodbye as she rose above the buildings and trees. She cast a warming spell over her and soon fell asleep. It had been a long day.

She awoke with a jolt on the soft grass of Pittsburgh's Frick Park as dawn broke. The bats hastily fluttered away. She scrambled down, found her way to the street, and flagged down an automobile. Since she was still wearing her red string bikini, she quickly secured a ride with a gray-haired salesman in a red BMW. They conversed about many tedious topics.

"Unseasonable weather we're having."

"That's Pittsburgh for you."

"Are you visiting or here on business?"

"I'm in sales."

"Seems you might have an interesting business."

"Not really dressed for the weather, are you?"

"Are you a Steelers fan?"

He did most of the talking.

He dropped her off at her family's home in the South Side. Her family was waiting impatiently outside their small brick house. She waved goodbye to her cheerful chauffeur.

"What took you so long?" demanded her mother.

"Well, there were these rats, cats, and bats..."

"Never mind. Come inside and change into something decent."

Wanda growled at her. Wilma giggled.

She followed her mother and sisters into the house, avoiding the glaring eyes of her sisters. After she changed into more appropriate dark clothing, they went into the family room and gathered around a boiling cauldron. The old familiar smell of dead newt and hemlock burned her sensitive nostrils.

Her mother said, "Now we cast the Strong Sister Spell to save our family business. Let us begin."

They formed a circle around the cauldron.

Wendy's mind drifted as they chanted. She could be on a runway strutting her stuff somewhere else instead of doing this nonsense. She could be hobnobbing with celebrities. She could be shopping in exotic stores or soaking up the sun on a remote beach. If she had any money, of course. She tried to concentrate on the spell, but her heart wasn't in it.

The next day a superstore popped up near their little shop of witchcraft accessories and vaping products and promptly undersold them.

Her mother threw Wendy out of the house and her sisters teamed up to cast an ugly spell on her. She left in humiliation but couldn't blame them.

She figured she'd apply to be a greeter at that new store.

# The Pixie Barter

## S. Cameron David

Sophia had no place among the learned people of the world. In all her thirty-eight years of life, never once had she seen inside a university's lecture halls or stepped foot within a merchant's mansion. She had little wealth and no reputation beyond the reach of her village roads. But that was fine. It was a fate she'd accepted long ago. She had her work to sustain her, and that was enough.

And so this village healer sneaked through the forest, clutching a glass jar at her hip, creeping about the mushrooms and toadstools, and the scattered herbs and lichens. She danced her way past gnarled roots as they wound between the trees. She leapt through a curtain of moss that fell suspended from the branches, landing soft-footed in a moonlit glade.

The clearing was practically empty, save for Sophia and her would-be prisoner.

She breathed a sigh of relief, spotting a faerie asleep in a briar's bloom, casting a faint luminescent glow. The flower had been torn off its stem and set down on the yellow grass. Each of its petals was soaked in honey (for the pixies were known to very much love the scent of honey, just as they loved to rest in their flower beds).

And carefully, ever so carefully, Sophia tip-toed across the clearing to approach her faerie trap. One hand inched toward the flower while the other held up the open jar. Ever so slowly, she took flower and faerie together in her fingers. And then, her heart a jackrabbit behind her ribs, she brought forth the jar and tossed faerie and flower together inside, then gripped the stopper and slammed it shut.

Sophia took a moment to calm her racing pulse, even as she studied the pixie, watching it ricochet to and fro, crashing helpless against the glass.

A face flashed through her thoughts, carrying with it the image of a feverish young girl, consigned to her bed with a broken leg as a gangrenous infection raced toward her heart.

The healer bowed her head. "My name is Sophia. Would you treat with me, faerie?"

The pixie ceased its wild darting, and descended back to its bed of petals. Calmness settled over it once again. Its face turned upwards to catch Sophia's gaze. It did not open its mouth; rather, Sophia heard a quiet, lilting voice speaking inside her head.

"Would you free me, human?"

"If that would be the price of your assistance," Sophia answered aloud.

She heard soft pitched laughter. Amusement and cruelty sounded equally mixed.

"You misunderstand. For such a price, I'd forget this indignity. I'd not call on the Redcaps to bring me your head."

"Then I suppose we're at an impasse."

The faerie smiled. "I suppose we are."

Then back they went, the wise woman, the jar, and the faerie inside the jar. Back through the woods and into the village—back into a gloomy room in a gloomy house where a child lay murmuring in her bed, suspended somewhere in the borderland between life and death, between sleep and hallucination.

"She won't last much longer," Sophia said, setting the jar beside the girl. "Her sickness lies far beyond my skill to treat. I was hoping you'd have the power to restore her..."

She swallowed, as tension knotted through her like coiling snakes. She had hoped that a faerie might achieve what she could not, but what did Sophia know of faerie magic with its potential limitations?

But when the faerie spoke, the snakes inside her uncoiled and departed.

"I suppose I can. Assuming you would pay the price."

"Anything."

The pixie snorted, unimpressed. "Never be so free with your offers. There are those of us who'd take all you possess, leaving only your bones for the Earth."

The pixie then turned its attention to the child, studying her from the other side of the glass. "She is half-claimed by death already. Another day or two, and she'd be beyond even my ability to save." It paused, quirking its head. "A life for a life. I suppose that's the usual way of these things."

Sophia could not say she was surprised. Miracles tended to exact a heavy price. "So, I would die in her place."

"And would you pay that price? She is not your child after all. You are of no relation."

"And that matters?"

"In Faerie, relations are everything. Blood ties and family most of all."

"You don't understand."

"No," said the faerie. "Then again, I suppose that doesn't matter. Would you pay such a price if it was what was what I asked?"

Sophia looked back towards the child, feverish and near to death. So young and innocent, with so many years to live.

"Yes."

"You are a strange one."

"I have a duty."

Her words were answered with a smile. "I think I like you," the pixie declared. It paused, as if struck by a thought. "Five years: this is my offer. Five years of your life, to be given to Death in the child's stead. Then both you and the child can live a while longer. And you will free me from this jar."

Sophia did not hesitate. She uncorked the stopper, and the faerie burst free in a blaze of light, forcing the healer to shut her eyes. When they opened again, the faerie was gone, and the child breathed easier as her fever began to subside.

Sophia trudged away, feeling newfound aches in her back and knees, carrying a few new wrinkles and a great many new gray hairs. But were she to look into a mirror—were she to see those signs of aging written stark across her face—she'd have been contented all the same.

She had no use for vanity or halfhearted regret. She had her work to sustain her.

And that was enough.

# FOR THE BIRDS

## *Pamela Love*

Ever wonder what would happen if you crossed firecrackers with feather dusters?

Me neither. So you can imagine my surprise yesterday when I was eating a sandwich beside a peaceful country road and suddenly—*squawk!* Birds were everywhere—dozens of different kinds, all squabbling with each other. Feathers were flying—some without birds attached.

Dodging behind a tree, I wiped sweat off my forehead. "Whew! What's the trouble?"

Expecting no answer, I was startled to hear one. "They're fighting over who makes the sweetest music. Fine way to prove it, right?"

I turned around. "How do you—no!" My jaw dropped. (That was a mistake. Another feather came zipping by which I almost swallowed.) Perched on a branch was a talking crow.

He laughed as I coughed on a quill. "You've whistled bird

songs up and down this road so long we can understand each other." (True. I'm a peddler.) Crow nodded toward the battling birds. "*Such* harmony." He shook his head.

Without thinking, I pulled out a whistle I use to scare off dogs and the occasional dragon and blew a piercing blast. "That's enough! Let *me* decide who makes the sweetest music."

Moments later, the birds had settled down, all staring at me.

"You'll be sorry," said Crow. "They already asked me to judge. Everyone knows nothing's sweet about me, least of all my voice, so I could be fair. I refused."

"Why?"

"Wait and see." The black-feathered bird fidgeted. "But do your best. Humans started this nonsense, so a human should end it.

"Yesterday some people came by in a wagon, playing flutes and fiddles. They stopped to listen to our songs, then started arguing about which of us was best. When they left, they hadn't made up their minds."

Robin hopped forward. "We've been fighting off and on ever since. But you know our music, Peddler. Which bird's is sweetest?"

"Better make up your mind by tomorrow morning," said Crow. "Our chicks will start hatching in the afternoon."

"Yes, yes! We must be there when they do," the rest chorused.

"Let me think," I said. Which made every bird start singing at once, as loud as they could. Honestly, it sounded worse than their quarreling.

When I stuck my fingers in my ears, Crow took the hint.

Or maybe he just felt sorry for me. Anyway, he organized the "auditions" so at least they sang one at a time. First Nightingale, then Wood Thrush, and on and on. Hours went by. My eyes were glazing over. *I never knew how many songbirds there are.*

It wasn't just songs, either. Woodpecker drummed away with his beak on a pine tree, and Hummingbird hovered next to my ear, which made an elegant tune in its own way.

It was well past sunset by the time everyone had taken their turn. I held up a hand. "Let me sleep on it. I'll decide in the morning." Folding my pack for a pillow, I lay down, grateful for silence at last.

"Wake up, peddler!" I managed not to groan. "I am Nightingale, the finest singer of all."

"I heard you this morning."

"Bah!" The bird snorted. "That was my brother. I am far more talented."

"Please, let me sleep." I rolled over.

Nightingale flew away with ruffled feathers, muttering words that were anything but sweet.

I had just nodded off when something shrieked in my ear. I practically took flight myself, I jumped so high. "What! Help!"

"It's me, Screech Owl. Isn't my voice memorable?"

My heart was pounding. "I'll never forget it."

"Splendid! Want to hear an encore?"

"No, please. I need a good night's sleep to make my decision."

"You can't fall asleep now. My cousins are on their way: Barn Owl, Spotted Owl, Great Horned Owl..."

I gritted my teeth. It was going to be a long night. But I had to be fair, so I wrapped my arms around my knees and listened until the owls had finished their concert and I could doze off.

It seemed like minutes later—maybe it *was* only that long, there were *so many* owls—before Rooster woke me at dawn. I yawned. By this point, I could hardly remember which music belonged to which bird.

Then one I hadn't seen the day before fluttered up to me. "I'm Mockingbird. I should win since I can mimic all the others." She proceeded to prove it, which meant hearing every single song all over again.

One by one, the other birds landed nearby. From their grumbling, it was clear they agreed on one thing at last—they were furious with Mockingbird.

Finally I interrupted her mid-solo to beg for one last minute of peace. I trudged off, wishing I'd stayed out of the birds' business. *No matter which I choose, there will be trouble.*

Bobolink landed in a roadside ditch. "I've already heard you sing," I reminded her.

"I'm lining my nest," she said, plucking blades of grass. "My chicks will need a soft bed." She left, her beak full.

Groaning, I clapped my hands over my face. *How will the losers' chicks feel when they learn about this? And how conceited will the winner's chicks become? Almost as conceited as I was, thinking I could solve this problem easily—oh!*

I had it. Running back to the birds, I sat down cross-legged. "Friends, I don't need to give you an answer."

"Couldn't make up your mind, could you?" Crow asked with a sneer.

I shrugged. "Why should I? You birds already chose the winning music yesterday." They twittered in confusion. "What do I mean? Well, why do you need the answer now?"

"Because it's almost hatching time!"

I grinned. "Is there a sweeter sound than your chicks breaking out of their shells?"

But to me, the sweetest sound was the cheering of the birds, even Crow.

# FUTURE SOLUTION

## *Garry Engkent*

In 40,004 BC, Ugh was searching for food at the base of a hill when he saw the cave ,where things were tumbling down. His eyes could not identify these items, but his nose smelt sweetness and nutrients. He took something. His tongue tasted strange flavors alien to his palate. Then he ate until his belly was bulging. Ugh would share this plenty with his tribe. Haa, the gods have answered their prayers!

Then he entered deep into the cave. Along the way, it was chock full of wondrous things, both edible and inedible, beyond his imagination.

At the other end, he heard gods and goddesses speak in strange tongues. From their smiles, Ugh knew the divine ones were pleased. There was jocularity in their voices, a merriment in celebration. Truly, they were mighty gods that the elders spoke of. Ugh was in rapture as he took another sample of the gods' generosity from the pile, returned to his side of the cave, and could not wait to tell everyone what he had found.

Before Ugh was beyond the voices of divinity, he heard but did not understand, "I told you this time portal is useful to dump waste!"

# Bird Brain

## *Mike Murphy*

Even deep into his favorite ornithological book, which lay open on his lap, Terwilliger noticed the pregnant brunette sit down beside him on the park bench.

"Good afternoon," she said.

"Afternoon," he replied.

She held out a dainty hand with painted black fingernails. "Rhea Craig."

"Herman Terwilliger," her bench mate replied, shaking the hand gently.

"Lovely day."

"Yes."

She glanced at his book. "You're a birder?"

"Have been for years," Herman answered. "You?"

She smiled and gently rubbed her belly. "I'm pretty busy for a hobby right now."

"Maybe later."

"What kinds of birds do you see up here? Anything unexpected?"

Herman sighed. "Sadly, no. Lots of robins, blue jays, chickadees, grackles. I have several feeders in my yard, but they seldom attract anything rare – even with the priciest of seed."

"Have you ever seen a blue tit?"

"A few years ago, when I vacationed in England."

"No, I meant *here.*"

"In Massachusetts?" he asked, trying not to chuckle at the suggestion. "They'd be *way* off course."

Rhea leaned closer to him. "I'll bet you twenty dollars," she said, "that you'll see one today."

Herman flipped through the pages of his book. "Of course I can see one," he said. "There's a picture of –"

"Not a picture," she clarified. "A living, breathing bird."

"When?"

"Soon," Rhea answered. "You know their colors, of course?"

Terwilliger was eager to share his knowledge. "Oh yes: Yellow, green, white –"

"Do we have a bet?"

Herman wondered what Rhea was up to. Did she think him an easy mark? Twenty bucks was a small price to pay for such a sighting; the gang at his birders' club would never believe him.

"Well?" Rhea asked again.

"I'm. . . I'm not sure."

"Too much?"

"No," he assured her. "What do I get if the bird doesn't show?"

"He will."

"But..."

"I'll leave you alone to enjoy your book," she answered.

"What do you say?"

"OK," Terwilliger agreed.

When he reached for his wallet, Rhea said, "Not now. When I've earned it."

Herman flipped to the blue tit's picture in his book. His mind wandered – lost in the many European vacation bird sightings – when he heard Rhea. "There!"

Terwilliger returned to the present and the inexplicable sight of a male blue tit just feet from him. "Incredible!" he said excitedly, but not so much as to scare away the visitor. "How did you –"

Rhea quietly shushed him, a pointy, black-nailed finger against his lips. "Just enjoy its visit."

After a few minutes, the tit flew away. "Was it worth twenty dollars?" Rhea asked.

"Absolutely!" Herman took out his wallet and removed four five-dollar bills. As he handed them to Rhea, the bird returned and gently perched on her shoulder.

Rhea, money in hand, slowly collapsed into herself – as though she was swirling down a drain. Amid a flash of sunlight, she morphed into a female blue tit, her fingernails now talons. For a moment, she and her mate sat cooing on the bench. Terwilliger was tempted to reach out and touch them.

With the five-dollar bills firmly in the female's beak, the two birds flew high up and into their tree nest. Herman watched as much as he could, but his eyes had known better days. He put his book down, stood, and peered upward. The birds were using the notes to strengthen their home.

A glance at his watch showed Terwilliger it was time to leave. Mr. Billings wouldn't be happy if he was late returning from lunch. He squinted at the high-up nest and smiled like he hadn't in several years. He pulled his coat tight around him and bent to retrieve his book.

The volume, which he *knew* he had closed when he stood, was open to the section about the tit. In the crease between the pages lay a small, blue feather. He delicately put it into his shirt pocket, concluding it was Rhea and her mate's way of saying thank you.

Terwilliger tucked his book under one arm and left the park to the unmistakable sound of blue tit trills.

# Siren's Younger Sister

## *Jeanna Mason Stay*

Kalina sighed as another ship approached the island. A little closer, and her sister would start singing. She gathered a few dozen earplugs and boarded her rescue boat.

The haunting music began drifting over the waves, and the ship staggered in the water. It veered suddenly, rushing toward the rocks surrounding the island. Kalina was already navigating her own boat through the treacherous waters toward it. By the time she got to the foundering ship, it had crashed, and passengers were thrashing in the waves.

Ligeia stopped singing. She usually only cared about the performance, rarely watching the aftermath. Kalina threw out her life preservers and dragged the survivors onto her boat, giving them earplugs anyway, just in case.

She heaved a dark-haired man onto the deck and checked his pulse. His heartbeat was steady, and he didn't seem injured, so she'd almost moved on to the next victim when he opened his eyes. They were a lovely deep green. He blinked at her silhouette, backlit by the afternoon sun. "Mermaids?" he asked feebly, then fell unconscious.

Kalina rolled her eyes. Humans were so predictable.

Hours later, Kalina had settled everyone into neat rows of cots and attended to the injured. The green-eyed man still slept, and she inspected him more closely. She'd seen her share of handsome men, but she didn't mind seeing another.

As if he felt her eyes, he woke, looked straight at her, and groaned. "Ergh, what happened?" He rubbed his forehead. "Did I call you a mermaid?"

"It's a pretty common reaction."

"I blame my sisters. We watched a lot of Disney."

*Not the worst thing you could blame a sister for*, she thought. "My name isn't Ariel."

He chuckled. "So what is it?"

"Kalina," she said.

"Aaron."

"Nice to meet you."

"Thanks for saving me." He groaned again, and Kalina reached for a bottle of painkillers. "So, what *did* happen? I just remember music... and then chaos."

Kalina liked this one, so she decided to tell him the truth. "You fell victim to my sister, Ligeia. She's a siren—like from mythology. She sings, you crash, I rescue. It's kind of our thing."

Aaron stared. Finally, he said, "You're kidding."

"Nope."

"That's... unexpected." He winced again. "Pretty close to mermaids, though."

The next few days were far nicer than she was used to

after a shipwreck. Aaron chatted with her as she helped the others, and he recovered quickly and began helping too. It was pleasant, and he was funny, and she found herself, against her better judgment, falling in love.

"You ever think about leaving the island?" Aaron asked.

Kalina grimaced. "I'm bound here with Ligeia. Neither of us can leave. I can barely get past the rocks to save the shipwrecks. Trust me, I've tried. But it's not so bad. I have a magical ship to send back our victims; I've got a fulfilling career helping others; I've got beach hair women would kill for."

He laughed, a sound Kalina was growing to love. "How do you know so much about the rest of the world?"

"Google, of course."

"You have internet?"

"Doesn't everybody?"

"It gets through your magical barrier?"

"It's tricky, and I've had to work a lot of tech mumbo jumbo with some washed-up electronics, but yeah, I can get a signal." She shook her head in despair. "Not enough to stream *The Mandalorian*, though."

"Tragedy."

Bit by bit, Kalina and Aaron learned about each other's lives. Kalina's sister was a prima donna who loved having an audience, even if it killed them. Aaron was a director doing small-time work for a big TV company. He finally brought up the subject they'd both avoided. "I have to leave eventually," he said.

She frowned. "I know."

"But I'd like to come back."

Her eyes darted to his in hope until she remembered. "You

107

can't. Once you pass the magical barrier around our island, you forget everything." She took a breath. "You'll forget about me."

An idea came to her a few days later as he explained the recording equipment he'd brought on the ship, parts of which had washed ashore. It probably wouldn't work, but it was the best chance they had. She stewed over it another day as she repaired his recording equipment. It was crucial to the plan.

"Will it work?" he asked.

"Honestly? I don't know. But it's all I can think of." She looked away, uncertain. "It requires a lot from you. You'll have to do all the convincing. And the remembering."

He smiled reassuringly. "I will *not* forget you. As for the convincing? That's my job."

She smiled too, hiding her sadness and fear. According to the plan, he'd be leaving in a few days, maybe forever.

Two months later she woke to an unexpected but hoped-for sound. It hit her like a ton of bricks. A ship, sailing carefully through the rocks, even though Ligeia was singing. Could it be?

She ran to the shore to find workers with earplugs already unloading huge boxes. She scanned the faces for one in particular.

"You came back," she yelled.

He removed his earplugs and met her halfway across the sand. "Of course."

"The recording worked!" They'd spent several days recording endless details of the island to help him remember it once he'd left.

"The pitch worked too! Your island is now a destination

for next season's *Reality Shipwreck Island*." His gaze warmed her skin. "The contracts will be ridiculously complicated, and the broadcast will be tough, but I told them I knew someone who could work the tech." He winked.

She smiled. It sounded amazing, and she thought even Ligeia would love it. Millions of listeners every week. Good thing recording canceled out her voice's power.

"And guess who's going to direct?" He pointed to himself. "Looks like I'll be sticking around."

Her smile widened, and she put her arms around his neck. "That's music to my ears."

# THE HUNT(ERS)

## *Tom Folske*

"Whoo-wee!" Zacharia Hix hollered, cheering his beer with his two hunting buddies: Hank Mackeroy, and Carl Stout. All three men were gathered around a small fire, warming their fingers in its soft glow, and talking about kills both past and present.

"Good job taking down that buck today," Carl said as he patted Zacharia on the shoulder. "A ten pointer, you should damn near get that thing mounted."

"I know, I was thinking about it . . . I still can't believe we've all killed a deer already and it's only our third day in. Usually, I'm lucky to even see one this early," Zacharia replied.

"Maybe the 'squatches stopped eating 'em," Hank said, then looked at Zacharia deviously. "Maybe they found themselves something tastier to eat." His tone of voice was a bit creepy, given how deep they were within the woods.

"What are you talking about?" Zacharia asked.

"Oh nothing . . . " Hank answered. "It's just an old Native

American legend that there are bigfoot in these parts. I mean it's probably just something they say to spook all the white hunters, but you never know."

Hank tried to present himself in a way that seemed ominous or half-joking, but Zacharia thought that he believed in what he was saying, probably more than just a little bit.

"Sleep with one eye open," Carl said, joining in with a booing sound like a ghost, breaking the odd tension that seemed to have been on the horizon.

Everyone laughed, and as they finished a couple more beers, they forgot about the legend completely.

They were just about to pack up for the night when there was a loud sound from directly behind them. Zacharia jumped up and spun around just in time to see a gargantuan, fur-covered, humanoid ape-beast come bursting full speed out of the forest, heading right for him. He didn't even have time to realize that he was being attacked before his jaw was shattered by the creature's giant swinging fist.

Zacharia fell to the ground dazed, bleeding, and in intense pain, watching as Carl started to run, only to trip over and tangle himself in his tent. Hank made for his rifle, picked the weapon up, fumbled with it in his trembling hands for a second or two, then dropped it to the ground again as the creature rushed forward and took his face between its mammoth hands.

Carl evacuated his bowels as he scrambled to his feet again. He started to run, but collapsed again immediately; it looked as though he must have broken his ankle. He got up one more time and made it a few feet, briefly alternating between hobbling and crawling, before the sasquatch caught up to him. The monstrous creature easily lifted the injured hunter into the air, turning and breaking the man's spine effortlessly against a nearby tree. The creature made a noise eerily similar to laughter; Zacharia had never heard or experienced anything so terrifying in his whole life. The monster turned around and with a sinister, gluttonous, almost-human grin, began walking back toward him. Zacharia had never wished death upon anyone more than he wished it on himself in that very moment.

The enormous mother sasquatch roamed casually through the forest, leading her burgeoning adolescent back to their cave. When they got closer to their home, however, the large sasquatch began to smell smoke, and shortly after that, she began to hear voices off in the distance. She uttered a satisfied grunt of approval. There had been a lot of hairless ones in this area lately, the small, pink, hairless things that tasted a lot better than deer. The two bigfoots suddenly found themselves taking a small detour, one that just happened to lead in the direction of the light ruckus and distant firelight.

As soon as they encroached upon the hairless ones gathered around their flames, the mother paused and looked lovingly at her offspring, before backing out of the way entirely, giving him the privilege to do this one on his own. It was a rite of passage and the time had finally come.

The young sasquatch's face veritably formed into a smile that implied both honor and excitement. This was to be his first kill. Well, his first time killing one of them, and he wanted to impress his mommy so badly. He hugged his mother and rubbed his head and face against her chest in an oddly human display of affection, before turning around quickly and charging eagerly at the three pink animals they had snuck up on. A tear came to the mother sasquatch's eye as her beautiful boy made short work of the screaming hairless ones. She had never been so proud in her life.

# Harry's Hairy Situation

## *Guy Belleranti*

Harry Oldster's laughing fits began two days after his hair transplant.

"What's so funny?" snapped his wife Madeline.

Harry pointed at the top of his head.

"Oh, I get it," Madeline said, smiling. "You're laughing because you'll soon have thick curls covering your dome."

"No...no...ha...ha...hee!"

Madeline's smile twisted into a scowl. "What did you say?"

"Hee...heee...heeeee!" Again Harry pointed at his head.

Madeline crossed her arms across her stomach. "This isn't normal, Harry. I'm taking you back to Dr. Crabtree's clinic."

Harry laughed all the way. He continued laughing as they got out of the car and entered the clinic. When the pretty blonde receptionist greeted them, Harry laughed even harder. "I'll check if Dr. Crabtree can see you at once," she said, and ran through a back doorway. Dr. Crabtree could, and Harry and Madeline were escorted to an examination room.

"My goodness!" Dr. Crabtree exclaimed as he entered and saw Harry rolling on the floor in a giggling mass. The doctor straightened his wire-rimmed glasses on his beak-like nose, and then, as Harry rolled his way, he reached out quickly to touch Harry's scalp.

"Hmm." Dr. Crabtree dropped to his knees and scooted across the floor after the rolling, Harry, feeling and prodding the laughing man's head while at the same time trying to avoid Harry's flailing arms and legs.

"Hmm," the doctor murmured. "Hmmm. Hmmmm."

"Hmm, hmmm, hmmmm what?" demanded Madeline.

Dr. Crabtree scrambled to his feet and darted behind his desk as Harry rolled his way. "Hmm, hmmm, hmmmm we have here a most unique situation," he replied.

"Situation?" Madeline glared. "What do you mean? What's happening to my Harry?"

"Let me ask Harry a few questions first, Mrs. Oldster." Dr. Crabtree once more kneeled on the floor. "Harry, do you think you can answer my questions? Nod and blink your eyes fast for "yes". Shake your head and keep your eyes closed for "no"."

Harry rolled toward the doctor's desk, and nodded his head, blinking rapidly.

"Good. Here we go. Are you laughing because your head tickles?"

Harry nodded, blinked, giggled and rolled.

"Is the tickling coming from the inside...under your scalp?"

Harry nodded and blinked again, his giggles growing louder with each nod and blink.

Dr. Crabtree smiled. "That's what I thought." He turned back to Madeline. "It's Harry's hair transplant."

"What about it?" Madeline asked.

"Well, it's...uh..it's growing wrong."

"Wrong?"

"Yes. It's growing in rather than out. It's tickling every nerve in his head, tickling his brain, tickling, tickling, tickling. Most unique, just like I said."

"So what can you do? How can you stop it? How can you help my Harry?"

Dr. Crabtree pursed his lips. "Well, Mrs. Oldster, there's only, uh, one way. I need to, uh, unplant the transplant."

"But won't that hurt?"

"Oh, I'll sedate Harry first, of course. Let me call Nurse Nimble in for assistance, and then if you'll help me hold Harry while she gives him the shot...."

"Never saw anyone laugh so much while getting an injection," Nurse Nimble commented ten minutes and several rolling-across-the-room Harrys later.

"Indeed," Dr. Crabtree agreed. He smiled at Madeline. "Now, ma'am, if you'll be seated in the waiting room we'll soon have Harry returned to you as good as old."

"That'll be such a relief," Madeline said.

And it was. Madeline never again yearned to run her fingers through the locks of a hairy-headed Harry, and Harry never again groused about being bald. And that's the bald truth.

# THE FAIRY'S GAMBLE

## *Claire Davon*

Miriam took a deep breath and stepped off the cliff face.

If this failed, she was going to die.

Wind rushed past her as she gained momentum in her plunge to the distant water. Ten feet down and the lumps on her back stayed as they were. Inert, useless. Her brothers, sisters, all her family, jumped off this place a dozen times a week and never suffered consequences.

Fairies had wings for a reason.

She was falling fast, her hair and clothes streaming behind her. Her heart was hammering in her chest. This last, desperate attempt to get her body to behave meant she was going to be smashed to bits on the rocks below in a few short seconds. Her life was being measured in the strata of the land she was hurtling past, and soon would be no more.

Miriam plunged another ten feet. The waves were getting closer with every second. Even if her wings broke free and unfurled now, it wouldn't be in time. She'd doomed herself with this stupid escapade. Her sister's wings came out when she had almost been killed by a runaway car the last time they visited the mortal realm. The difference was, if Celia had been struck, doctors might have been able to save her. Miriam would not be saved after a fall like this. She was risking it all—and was going to lose.

Miriam had to do something. She couldn't be the one fairy in her family without wings. At twenty years old, she was well past the time they should have come out. Most emerged during puberty, and she'd been a woman for six years. If she didn't act now, she'd be shunted to the side, like the rest of the defective ones. Without hers, Miriam might be a member of the family, but she'd be like crazy Uncle Rigo, who was whispered about in corners and glimpsed at holidays.

When she'd gotten one more sorrowful look from her Great Aunt Elvenia, she'd decided to act. Recalling her sister's happy emergence, Miriam opted for a desperate action. Nobody could know or they would try and talk her out of it. The cliff was far too dangerous for those without the power to fly. Many ended their existence in the human place that was this equivalent.

The distance was two hundred yards from the top to the base, where rock shards and whitecaps waited. The ocean grew closer with each passing foot. She screamed, but the sound was snatched away.

She'd been so sure this drastic action would work. Now nothing was left for her but death. She'd end her life a crumpled body washed up on shore. She twisted and turned, but nothing would stop her downward trajectory.

Without warning, her wings burst free, the pain as they tore from her back nothing compared to the air cutting into her skin. The water was so near that damp coated her body, or maybe that was the fear of her impending death. Her brain was muzzy and light-headed, and she couldn't think of anything except the beautiful gossamer appendages that had appeared under such intense circumstances. Too bad she wasn't going to be alive long enough to enjoy them.

At this rate of speed, the ocean would be like cement, crushing her body and smashing her bones. She was still going to die, and what they would find was her broken, winged form. She'd be a fairy in all ways at the end, but a dead one.

The waves were so close now, death in their blue expanse. She glimpsed the beach where they liked to play and wished she were there now instead of here, where the dolphins and fish would be the ones to witness her demise. Should she put her arms out or keep them by her side? No matter how she tried to break her fall, it wouldn't make a difference. Death was all around her. A wave went high and the crest of it almost touched her.

Her body grazed the water, globules splashing over her torso and soaking her. Then she swept up and away, water streaming from her as she staggered up, out of danger. Drops fell back down to the lethal sea, returning to the brine that had almost taken her. Would have taken her, if her beautiful, wonderful wings had not emerged.

As she struggled upward, her still-damp wings sagging under her unfamiliar weight, she wondered if she was still doomed. She listed, her body shifting to one side and then sagging back in the direction of the sea. She cried out, her terrified shout lost to all but her ears. When she stabilized, Miriam dragged in a breath. Above her, someone jumped off the top—perhaps one of her sisters had discovered her whereabouts and joined her.

Whoever the person was, they would be too late.

Then she caught the wind and she soared upward. Her wings pulled on her back in a welcome tug. The pain was nothing compared to the exhilaration of success. Miriam would have danced for joy, if she'd been on the ground. She did so in the air, doing a ragged loop that showed ocean, then rock, then sky, then ocean again.

As the stranger got closer, Miriam made out Celia's smiling face. Miriam grinned back as she used her newfound appendages to struggle upward, against the wind.

Now that she had her wings, she'd be back to this place, this time as one of the family.

She had done it.

# ANOTHER UNIVERSE

## D. Thomas Minton

Sparks glittered across Rachel's amber eyes as she rotated the bottle in front of her face. "It's beautiful," she said. "What is it?"

Two weeks past, Ben had spotted the bottle in the trash can at the bus stop and thought it only a bottle of silver and blue glitter. As he waited, however, it had started to glow, not brought on by a parting of the clouds, but by an inner light wholly its own. When he fished it out from among the catsup-stained hamburger wrappers, the sparkles had danced forth like droplets of sunlight.

Ben swallowed the lump in his throat, conscious of Rachel's eyes watching him over the bottle's curve of glass. He wanted to say something witty. "Stars," he said instead.

Rachel cocked a perfectly sculpted eyebrow.

"In a bottle," he added, cringing. His gaze dropped to study the bottom of the Pyrex measuring cup nestled in his hands. He wanted a do-over, but he knew it was too late.

A week ago, last Thursday, Rachel had moved into the apartment across the hall. She lived with two other women -- all Phi-Beta-Kappa beautiful. This was the third time she had knocked on his door seeking an essential baking ingredient, this time, vegetable oil. "Brownies," she had explained, her sheepish grin sliding like sunshine over the top of the graduated cup she held up. "The chocolate kind."

Ben had forced a laugh and taken the offered measuring cup. Unexpectedly, Rachel had followed him into his apartment.

Awkward his entire life, Ben often felt inadequate at school, in life, at work, in love—not that he'd ever had the courage to ask a girl out for a scone and a cappuccino, except in his head. As a kid, his head had always been a better place to live; there, he made the gimme layup on the basketball court instead of passing the ball away so he didn't risk the disappointment of clanging it off the rim.

Artie, his co-worker at the Garlic Pit, insisted Rachel had a crush on Ben. "No one who bakes as much as Rachel allows her cabinet to run dry of vegetable oil, flour, or baking soda," he had observed while Ben chopped black olives for the chain's underwhelming puttanesca. Besides, Artie's reasoning continued, girls like Rachel ate baked goods on a decadal timescale, not tri-weekly. "Simple first order logic," he insisted.

Ben assembled his own first order logic: if Artie thought girls like Rachel crushed on guys like Ben, then Artie was an idiot.

Rachel shook the bottle, and pinpoints of light streaked across the apartment's bare eggshell walls and speckled her spaghetti-strap top.

"You mean, like a pocket universe?" Rachel's grin revealed neat rows of teeth. "Let's open it." She reached for the cork stopper.

"Don't!" Ben dropped the measuring cup as he half-reached for the bottle. Ashamed, he took longer than needed to corral the rolling glassware so he wouldn't have to look at her.

If she opened the bottle, whatever was inside might escape, like everything beautiful and magnificent seemed to do.

"What if it is another universe?" Rachel asked. "With another Rachel and Ben and a bottle just like this one? Only they open it." Rachel's eyes sparkled brightly with the same light that radiated from the bottle in her hands.

What if opening it could—

Ben shook his head at the thought.

Not in this universe.

Rachel's lids slid over her eyes, and the sparkle was gone. Her fingers brushed Ben's as she placed the unopened bottle into his hand.

Ben put it back on top of the TV from where Rachel had picked it up. "It's just—"

"It's okay."

But Ben could hear it wasn't.

He poured the oil into the measuring cup. After an awkward moment, she thanked him and closed the door behind her.

No, no, Rachel's dearth of fundamental ingredients was due to frequent baking--nothing else. That was the order of this universe.

Ben picked up the bottle and turned it in his hands. He couldn't see another Ben or Rachel in it, only pinpoints of light that didn't seem quite as beautiful now, as if some of their magic had bled away.

Was it another universe? Did it have another Ben in it who had taken that chance, not just in his mind, but in the real world?

Ben sighed. Even in another universe, he would probably do the same stupid thing again because guys like him weren't brave enough to take advantage of first, let alone second, chances.

"What have you got to lose?" Artie had asked last night while they waited beneath the flickering sodium glow of the streetlamp for their buses home. "Life is a poker game. When you go all in, maybe you end up walking home naked in the dark, but if you don't even try, then you're definitely sitting on the same old bus next to a guy that smells like cat food."

Simple first order logic: If Ben did nothing differently, then he was the idiot.

Ben wiggled the cork. It took some doing, but finally it—

A trillion billion suns rushed out.

"It's beautiful," Rachel said, sparkles glittering in her sweet blue eyes as she rotated the bottle in front of her face.

Ben felt a lump in his throat. He should offer a witty compliment, but what good would that do with a girl—

"Not as beautiful as you," he said, shaking off an odd sense of *déjà vu*.

# The Devil and Edgar J. Pattigan

## *Albert N. Katz*

Edgar Pattigan had made just the right type of wish that attracted Lucifer: he'd give his soul to the devil, if only his writing would be recognized as among the greatest works of literature ever produced.

You see, Edgar was a prodigious writer, albeit one who had difficulty in getting his short story collections and novels published by reputable publishing houses. "Too ahead of the curve," he comforted himself.

Self-published, he was faithfully followed by a select set of readers that bought enough of his output to pay for his hotdog-and-beans dinners and the sparce single room apartment he rented.

Edgar wanted more. Much more. But when he received his 1477th rejection letter, he made that fateful wish that brought Lucifer's number one soul-hunter, Beelzebub, to knock on his door with the promise that he'd grant the wish in exchange for his soul.

They haggled over terms. Edgar was determined not to let his soul go cheaply. He demanded that his oeuvre be recognized as the greatest writing of all time. Beelzebub countered. They went back and forth, until they agreed upon the following contract, signed, as per custom, in Edgar's blood: "Be it understood that in exchange for his soul, to be delivered on his death, the complete set of Edgar J. Pattigan's written novels and stories be recognized world-wide as among the greatest works of literature ever produced."

Edgar was satisfied. His works would be acknowledged as a worthy companion to those of Shakespeare, Tolstoy, and Cervantes!

Edgar started writing even more feverishly than he had before. Book after book, story after story was written but, despite his efforts, no lucrative contracts were offered and, sadly, his set of followers grew smaller with the death of one Irene Pinsky of Sioux Falls, South Dakota. Never faint of heart, Edgar kept on writing, kept on self-publishing until he had that predestined heart attack, and died in his one-bedroom apartment, face down in a plate of hotdogs and beans.

At the coal-black gates, Beelzebub was waiting to welcome him. Edgar Pattigan was livid. "You lied! You cheated me and didn't fulfill your part of the contract!"

Beelzebub lived for that moment when one of his clients experienced that moment of abject despair. Putting a sulphury arm around Edgar's shoulder, he explained that although he was, admittedly, the great deceiver, he was not a liar.

"Come," he said, "watch the world unfold as it will."

Being out of the linear constraints of time, Edgar watched and watched. He saw his time and culture fall into ruin, decay, neglect and soon forgotten. He saw new civilizations rise and fall as his once did.

Then another civilization arises, peopled by beings who shared only some of the hominid DNA that had run through his body. These were curious beings. A perfect meld of scientist and artist, their curiosity was unbounded. They explored. They investigated the past, the very distant past, until they came upon a simple abode of a primitive race. In that abode they found strange artifacts that took them years to decipher.

At this point, Beelzebub stopped the unfolding of time and whispered into Edgar's now burning ear, "I did that. I preserved only your writing to be found by these creatures. When they decipher it, they will recognize that this was the anonymous literature of a long-lost people and acknowledge it—as we had contracted—to be among the greatest works of literature ever produced, because, well frankly, they will have no other works from that period with which to compare it."

"But...but..." Edgar sputtered.

The demon smiled. "You will stay unknown, but your works will be admired worldwide. I didn't trick you. You tricked yourself by agreeing to the wording of the contract you signed." And with a theatrical laugh he cast Edgar into the inferno and pains that awaited him for eternity.

As is his wont, every two or three centuries Beelzebub checked how poorly his clients were faring. One after another he was delighted to find them even more miserable than they were on his previous visit, their lamentations ever louder. However, when he got to Edgar J. Pattigan he found him whistling happily as he swam in offal, blisters bursting and snakes eating his rotting body. Beelzebub prodded Edgar with his Staff of Woe, and to his chagrin it had no effect. Edgar seemed quite content. Confused Beelzebub confronted the human. "Why are you not in the pit of misery like those around you?"

"Because" replied Edgar, "you fulfilled the contract we had agreed upon."

This confused Beelzebub even further. "You idiot! You never achieved fame, nor fortune, and adoration. You lived a squalid life and died in obscurity. "

Edgar just smiled, "Indeed I did. But you never understood, did you, that all I ever wanted was to give joy to a large, and appreciative world-wide readership. And that you have given me."

Worried now that Lucifer would punish him for this error, Beelzebub muttered, "There is no way I could have known."

"Oh, but there was. If you had done your homework and read my books, you would have realized I negotiated our contract exactly as did my protagonist in my story, *The Trickster*, I haggled, suggesting that I wanted personal glory, which in fact, I did not. The words on the contract you thought pulled the wool over my eyes are exactly those used by my protagonist to trick the devil and obtain the one thing that really mattered to him. To bring joy through his words."

And then with a laugh that would have chilled Beelzebub's blood, if in fact he had blood, Edgar crowed, "Just as somewhere, sometime, I am doing."

# THERE IS NO RULE WITHOUT AN EXCEPTION

## *Lana Nizhehorodova*

It was a hot summer day, and Johnny was reading his favorite book in the attic. His parents went to the market, and the whole house was at his disposal, but he loved to spend his days in the attic. He loved it there because it was the only place in the house where he could be completely alone and do whatever he wanted.

He knew other kids liked to play outside, but Johnny had never been like them – he never liked loud games or noisy places. To Johnny, books were his world. His favorite book was about a spirit named Benjamin, who lived in the chimney and helped people who were in need. In the stories that Johnny liked best, Benjamin would whisper to an old woman and remind her where she put her money; in other tales, Benjamin would sew a scarf for a poor child or help a lost traveler find his way home.

As Johnny read about Benjamin's good deeds, he thought how great it would be to have him for a friend. Johnny didn't have many friends, and Benjamin seemed to be exactly the friend he wanted. As soon as this thought crossed his mind, he suddenly heard a noise in the old wooden wardrobe behind him.

Johnny stood up and opened it. To his total surprise and amazement, he saw Benjamin sitting inside; wearing a red costume, exactly as he had always imagined him to look.

"Hi, Johnny," the spirit said. "You didn't have a chimney, so I chose another place to live." He smiled at the boy and reached out his hand.

Johnny smiled back and took Benjamin's hand. "Oh, that's fine; make yourself at home," he said and added feeling a little shy, "Do you want to come and play with me? We can play chess; do you like that?"

Johnny went to the table and set up the chess board, still not believing how quickly his wish to be friends with Benjamin came true.

Johnny was so happy, and he and Benjamin became good friends. They spent a lot of time in the attic, reading, playing board games, or talking about their dreams. Benjamin was also 10 years old, just like Johnny, and the boys got along very well. At night Benjamin went away to help other people in need, but every morning he was back in the wardrobe, waiting for Johnny to share his adventures with.

It went on like that, and before long, summer ended; the air got chilly, and October was suddenly there. All the children in the neighborhood started to get ready for Halloween. They laughed and talked about what their costumes were going to be. Every house had pumpkins on the front stoop and the children were busy making jack-o'-lanterns. Johnny had heard when he was younger that carved pumpkins protected houses from ghosts. They were there to keep the spirits away. One afternoon on the way home from school the neighbor's children asked Johnny how many jack-o'-lanterns he was making. Johnny didn't know what to say. He knew that if he made even one jack-o'-lantern, Benjamin wouldn't be able to come back to his house ever again.

He stopped and without thinking about it said, "I have a spirit friend who lives in my attic, so I can't carve any this year."

To his surprise, the children didn't ask to meet Benjamin, but laughed instead. "That's dumb," one of them said. "Besides everyone knows spirits are evil and need to be chased away."

"But Benjamin isn't like that; he is a good spirit, and he helps people," Johnny tried to explain, but the children didn't listen. They made fun of him and ran home.

After that, the neighborhood kids didn't play with Johnny anymore. They called him strange, creepy and other names. Johnny was upset and he didn't know what to do. He didn't like everyone thinking he was weird. He really liked Benjamin. He was feeling conflicted.

Johnny's mother saw how sad he was and asked him what was wrong. He'd never told his parents about Benjamin because he was afraid they wouldn't believe him. But on that day he was very unhappy, and he decided to finally share his secret. He told his mother about his friend and how the other children were calling him names.

She sighed and asked him, "Do you like Benjamin?"

"Yes, I do. I like him a lot, he's a good spirit and he's my friend," Johnny said. "But I don't want everyone to think I'm strange. I just don't understand what to do. Should I make jack-o'-lanterns and maybe lose my friend, or not?"

Johnny's mother smiled and said, "In this life, Johnny, you've got to look with your own eyes and not only listen to what others say. You've got to stand up for those you love and care for. Friendship is a precious gift that needs protecting. So don't listen to what they say. You've got a real friend, and you know he is a good boy, and that's what matters."

Johnny listened and smiled at his mother. He was so glad that she understood, and he realized he had a wise and great mother. He kissed her cheek, looked out the window at all the pumpkins in front of the other houses and shrugged. He'd made his decision and went back to the attic to play with his good friend Benjamin.

# NEW OCCUPANT

## *Steven Streeter*

It was one of the storm-wracked nights that too often hit the town of Bournewith, set on the Atlantic coast of Cornwall, not far from Newquay, but far enough. A small place, more than four hundred years old by all records, said to have been the home of wreckers, men who would shine lamps on nights such as this to cause the wooden vessels to be shattered against the rocky shore. But the vessels were no longer made of wood, their sea-lanes did not pass so close to the coast, and with that illegal line in wealth procurement gone, Bournewith was dying a slow and gradual death.

It felt like a graveyard where the dead did not know they were dead yet.

It was in the late afternoon before this wild night that the large van pulled up in front of the old Potter house, followed by a brand new car. For years the Potter family had lived there, but when old Bessie Potter died an unloved and unmourned spinster, it was put up for sale, and had remained on the market for over a decade. Mr. Robinson, the realtor who came from somewhere out of town, stepped out of the new car and ran to the front door. He fumbled with a set of keys and eventually opened it, the door protesting loudly at being moved like this. Only then did the two men leave the van and slowly, but surely, unload minimal furniture and a lot of wooden crates into the house.

People stood in doors or peered through windows to see who the new neighbor was who had come to this place that usually only saw people leave.

The car that eventually pulled up was an antique, driven by a small man with the palest white skin. He drove into the driveway of the new house and hustled inside, his scrawny body swimming in a dark suit, his completely bald head quickly becoming rain-soaked, his sunken eyes looking haunted and yet eager. He disappeared inside and . . . nothing.

Everyone watched, though nothing continued to happen. Then the two men re-appeared, went back to the van, threw things inside, locked it up and it was soon gone. Less than an hour and all had been unloaded. Not long after them, Mr Robinson also left, looking rather pleased with himself.

The Potter house remained dark. No movements could be seen in windows, no sounds came out. Just as it had always been.

People were really curious now, but the storm was getting worse, and so none dared venture forth to see who this strange new arrival could be.

Evening fell. Two lights flickered in a window, small dots of orange, glowing eyes behind the threadbare curtains that had remained in place since long before Bessie Potter had finally died. Eyes that stared out at whatever they could see . . .

And that was when the clap of thunder and burst of lightning came together, bringing with it the full fury of the storm and taking the power in an instant, plunging Bournewith into complete, inky darkness.

Seen by only a few, the new stranger appeared in the door of his newly acquired house, smiled, and then disappeared back inside.

Fears increased; what sort of a man would relish weather such as this?

To make it worse, moments later, he was outside, one of the wooden crates on an old but very solid wheelbarrow. He struggled a little, but he walked stubbornly through the pelting rain, leaning into the wind with what seemed to be unnatural strength.

He went to the nearest house.

The residents shuddered under his approach.

He walked up the path and rapped his knuckles on the door.

They could not pretend to be away; their presence had been made obvious by their viewing of his arrival only hours before. With great reluctance and after a great length of time, the father opened the door.

The old man smiled, his yellowed teeth showing clearly. "Yes?" the father asked, trying to put on a brave face.

The old man opened his crate a fraction. "Jack Dowling, candle salesman," he said, maintaining his grin as he pulled out one of his wares. "Can I interest you in . . . ?"

# THE SEAHORSE

## *Conrad Gardner*

On a Thursday afternoon in the middle of May, Paul Robinson was sick. Of course, nothing about this event seems unordinary, but Paul would continue to vomit on and off over the following days. He visited the toilet more than usual and had a constant yawn. After two weeks of vomiting episodes and excessive toilet trips, his partner said, 'Maybe you're pregnant.'

They both laughed about it, but an uncomfortable idea entered Paul's mind. To get himself out of this funk, he visited a doctor.

The waiting room stirred unusual feelings within him. Two mothers played with their toddlers, who were sharing a set of blocks. The kids seemed... sweet to Paul, endearing, even. The doctor came and called him through, and Paul stole another look at the infants.

'So, Mr Robinson, you've been vomiting and urinating a lot?' Dr Hale said. Paul nodded. 'Anything else? Fatigue, maybe?' Paul joked that he always felt tired; it didn't land. 'Do you have any other observations that might be linked to this... episode?'

Paul opened his mouth to say no when he detected a wetness in his chest, against his shirt. It was stained by the nipples. The substance dripped down his chest.

Dr Hale gasped. A cleared throat later, the doctor leaned forward. 'Would you be comfortable with me performing a test on you, Mr Robinson?'

'Would you take a seat here?'

'Could you please unbutton your shirt?

'Are you comfortable with me shaving your stomach?'

An operator applied a gel against his abdomen, a slippery substance that didn't stick like one might expect. The operator and Dr Hale shared a look before placing the probe against Paul's skin. Paul turned away from the screen, and chose only to listen. The probe moved around a little and a soft thump sounded from the monitor. It grew clearer, had a beat to it. Paul didn't need to look at the screen; he could tell by the doctor's open mouth. His chest seemed to elevate and not release.

His partner took the news much better than expected. Beyond the queerness of it all, she said, she wanted to be a part of the child's life, if it was part hers. Paul didn't know who else could be the other parent. 'It's part of the deal,' she said. 'You know, like seahorses. They mate for life.'

It took Paul a couple of months to shave his body, but once he did, the stretching clothes were much smoother against his skin. He understood why Sarah wore leggings most of the time.

The morning sickness subsided, but he would've preferred it to the back pain and lactation.

'Hey, it's only six more months, right?' Sarah said.

He supposed she was right, but he hated the lingering eyes he received at work. Whenever he went outside his hands covered his stomach out of some paternal instinct.

A Tuesday morning the following February, Paul sat at his desk for work, when a wetness ran down his legs. Liquid dripped down his office chair and his heartbeat tripled its pace. The colleagues who were parents smiled more than those who weren't. Paul's boss, Miranda, drove him to the hospital while he called Sarah, and she met him there.

Paul explained that he was that Paul Robinson, that his water had broken via the anus. Dr Hale arrived seconds later. Paul consented to the use of anaesthetic after she told him that his urethra would shatter if he gave birth through it, and the process would involve an incision.

Paul's eyes opened on Sarah. Something had been applied to his stomach and it tingled. Sarah held a bundle in her arms. She brought it closer to him, and he looked into the eyes of their child, his child. He exhaled. That elevation in his heartbeat had disappeared, made lighter by those eyes, and he smiled.

# FACE TO FACE

## *Anne Karppinen*

The letterbox rattles; something unnaturally heavy hits the doormat. It's not even ten o'clock yet. I wiggle my toes and try to relax.

Minutes tick by, and I'm still awake. This body never ceases to confuse me; it doesn't feel like a finished concept. There are multiple design faults, and bits that seem like a waste of good human flesh. Toes, for example; they don't seem to do much. For that reason, they also amuse me the most. The Devil, as we know, is in the details.

While in possession of this body, I need to develop a personality – something potential customers can identify with. "Likes to wiggle toes" probably won't cut it in the interview. Specialisation is rare nowadays, and the fight for promotions harder.

I swirl these different reactions around in my head. The parcel on the doormat arouses a keen interest, which battles with inborn laziness. I asked for a placement in the North, thinking that it'd always be comfortably dark up here. Nobody cared to mention the lurid indoor lighting, or sunbeams shooting off freshly fallen snow. That's enough to make one's eyes water – and crying isn't really a part of my repertoire, either.

Still, it could be much worse. I could be working at some infernal call centre in India. At least here one is more or less independent. I wanted an opportunity to talk to people face to face; there's always a special kind of thrill when meeting a mortal body, and the immortal soul within. People blame us for every possible vice and absurdity there is: violence, tax returns, leggings. We'd love to take the credit – but alas, humans, in their infinite creativity, come up with these ideas without any help whatsoever.

There have been fewer contacts than I had hoped for. People walk past me, their heads down, their faces glued to a glowing screen. I tried the nightlife next, to slightly better success. For a while I thought that my work would be easy from then on.

During the intensive course, the overenthusiastic entity which went on about our "daily and weekly performance goals" and the "need to ramp up our human appeal" would sometimes mention in passing that secularisation "was still very much with us". I left the course thinking that it was much more of a problem for the other side – something that would play into our hands in the long run.

How wrong I was. In a multicoloured world the old black-and-white just doesn't cut it anymore. The line between good and evil is so tenuous that it's a hell of a job to keep track – and believe us, we've tried. No one is interested in counting angels on the head of a pin, or the circles of a standard-sized inferno. But start talking about the latest dieting fad, and everyone's all ears and unsolicited opinions. Or even better, show them a blinking screen and they'll stare at it, slack-jawed, for hours.

If only they would spend that time watching something truly corrupting – but no. Cute animals; short, monotonous songs; people having sex in repetitive, uninspiring ways. It didn't take me long to learn to appreciate the full meaning of the word 'mundane'.

I glance at the calendar hanging on the opposite wall. I can't stay in bed forever. Forever is a long time, and I'm painfully aware of that. I have more short-term goals to reach. By the early hours of the morning, I'll be able to bring home a semiconscious individual or two. There are always enough people who are up for a long weekend of drugs, muggings and a bit of random violence. Yet, when Monday morning rolls around, they'll inevitably return to their boring lives, donate money to a women's charity, or buy a well in Africa. Old-school repentance is rare. Money can buy everything, clean conscience included.

I've also tried the other route: offering people their heart's desire. In the old days most were content with a cartload of sausages, or a handful of coins. The playwrights and poets always went for the blue-eyed girl – or boy – next door. A drop of blood, a hastily scrawled signature and hey presto: a fresh soul all ripe for the sizzling.

What can I offer them now? Everything, from food to companionship, arrives at the touch of a screen. Why go through the trouble of flirting with eternal damnation, when you can just click a few boxes, swipe right, and key in your credit card number.

A bird lands on my windowsill, casually whistling a few shrill notes. I stare at it, but nothing happens. Smouldering glances are only for popular songs in this reality. I peer towards the door again. I rarely get mail, and the coal-black envelope finally pulls me out of bed. The logo is instantly recognisable: fiery red letters dancing on the corner of the envelope. The paper scorches my hands; the pages are glossy, and the print hellishly large.

*Dear esteemed DevilMayCare employee!*

*We are excited to welcome you into our dynamic F2F street marketing team! As your adjustment period is now over, we are expecting you to participate actively in our campaigning work full time.*

The text goes on: two pages of exclamation-filled phrases. Still, I don't let the style lead me astray; I know the realities of face-to-face marketing by now. From today onwards, I'm required to harvest five souls a week. Five hundred souls in three months, and one is automatically promoted. Fall short of the goal, and one's own existence will be on the line.

I take a deep breath and wiggle my toes. This is what I've been waiting for: a ticket from here to eternity. Working hard for said ticket goes against my very being, but in these circumstances one has to adapt. "No pain, no gain," is what the people here say – and downstairs it's always been pretty much the same ethos. Not even Hell can afford idle devils.

# Sir Blodry, the Hero

## *DJ Tyrer*

*The one problem with being acclaimed a hero*, considered Sir Blodry, *is that one was expected to* be a hero. And Sir Blodry knew, he was no hero.

It had all been an accident, a terrible accident. The dragon he'd been sent to slay had died through its own clumsiness, but everyone had assumed he'd killed it and that he was bold and brave. Which had been fine at first, as it meant feasting and gold and the attention of beautiful damsels.

Unfortunately, it also meant he got picked first when another quest presented itself and a daring knight was required.

Sir Blodry was not at all daring, but his protestations were taken as humility, and everyone cheered at how modest and brave he was and send him forth on an adventure; which was how he came to be sploshing his way through the sodden fenland in search of a troll. He had no idea what a troll was, merely that the priests and wizards of Arthur's court all agreed that it had come to Britain by clinging to the hull of a Saxon ship. He hoped he wouldn't find out anything more. But, as if summoned by his doleful thoughts, a large beast with the general form of a man and covered in either matted hair coloured green by moss or a tangled growth of swamp weed, rose from a miasmic pool and leered at him with sharp, yellowed teeth.

"Er, are you a troll?" asked Sir Blodry as he fumbled with his sword in an attempt to draw it forth from its scabbard.

The beast gurgled and roared at him, moistly. (It may well have been answering his query, but the knight didn't speak Trollish.)

Having finally drawn his sword, Blodry pointed the blade at it in an as unthreatening manner as a sharp blade can be pointed by a panicked knight.

The troll—, Blodry had decided it *was* a troll, made a sound that was probably a laugh.

Sir Blodry shook, and the sword wobbled in his hand.

"Look, if you're a troll, I have to smite you," he said. "I don't want to—I'd rather be somewhere warm and dry with something tasty to eat—but, I have to... alright?"

The troll made the sound again. The knight didn't feel at all confident.

"In fact," he said as it took a step towards him, "I really don't want to fight at all – bye!"

Sir Blodry turned and ran. Or, at least, sploshed, squelched and staggered as quickly as he could, the swampy ground sucking at his feet.

Taking long, loping strides, the troll followed just behind him, its wide, webbed feet just perfect in the fen environment.

Blodry didn't know what to do. He didn't dare stop and fight it, certain its size and strength would prove too much for him and knowing no other way to defeat it.

Moving slowly, he couldn't outpace it. Any moment now, he was certain, it would catch and devour him. Then, he saw the hut. It wasn't much, just a simple round hut on a low-lying hump of land with a roof bundled from dry reeds, but it meant someone else was there, and someone else might just have an idea what he should do.

With a cry, Blodry ran towards the hut. A door opened and an old woman stepped out.

"Who's making all that noise? Do be quiet, I just got my homunculus off to sleep."

She was, the knight realised, a witch. Whilst he'd prefer to avoid witches, and wizards, too, for that matter, there was a chance she would know how to handle a troll.

"Help me!" he cried.

Seeing the troll behind him, she gave a nod. The witch pulled out a wand, did a quick chant, and danced thrice about her hut (being a small hut, it didn't take long at all), then pointed her wand at him.

Sir Blodry felt himself changing. Then, he realised, he was a goat. He was a goat with large horns and an urge to butt the troll. Turning, Blodry charged at it. The troll made a sound of dismay and also turned around, allowing Blodry to butt it in the butt, sending it flying off across the marsh to land, entangled, in the bare branches of a dead tree.

The witch waved her wand and turned him back, saying, "The troll will painlessly evaporate in the sunlight and cause you no more trouble."

"The poor thing," said Blodry.

"It was going to eat you," the witch pointed out.

"I suppose so. Still, I'd rather have not troubled it at all."

"What a strange knight you are," she said, shaking her head.

"How did you know that turning me into a goat would work?" asked Blodry.

The witch laughed. "I'm from the Angle and everyone in the Angle knows the story of the goats and the troll. Of course, that was actually a bridge troll, but the principle's the same: Trolls cannot take a good butting."

Blodry shrugged, uncertain what she meant. Still, the troll was defeated, and he could go home a hero; so he thanked her and began to trudge his way back through the fens. The only problem, of course, was that when he told everyone he'd defeated the troll, nobody would want to hear about witches and goats... No, they'd just say how brave he was and send him off on another adventure. But, still, there'd be a victory feast first, at least. He loved a good feast.

# FORBIDDEN FRUIT

## *Tom Howard*

Selina placed her basket on the ground and unlocked the gate. Her mistress, Old Punca, had grown too feeble to harvest the dream fruit from the garden, so she sent the servant girl. Selina didn't mind. Harvesting the dream fruit took her away from scrubbing and cooking for the old witch. It wasn't a hard life. Old Punca rarely beat the girl for breaking crockery or scorching the gruel. The old woman spent most of the day in her rocking chair, nibbling dream fruit and smiling at nothing.

Fresh breezes blew through the nightshade outside the garden gate, and the path felt warm against Selina's bare feet. Inside the stone walls, strange trees of different shapes and sizes grew. Short or tall, wide-spread or twisted together, the trees stood row after row, their branches covered with small heart-shaped leaves in multiple colors. Selina locked the gate behind her. If Old Punca found it open, the servant girl would have no supper.

She searched for fruit hidden amidst the leaves. Small and

green meant the dream fruit had not yet ripened. Dreamers still nourished them. Round and red indicated mature dreams ready to pick. A black fruit meant a bad dream, or it had not been harvested in time. Selina didn't pick those.

She ran her hand over the soft skin of a plum-sized fruit, twisted it from its stem, and placed it on the linen in her basket. Bruising them ruined the dream, Old Punca said. Selina didn't know. She wasn't allowed to taste them. Even the overripe ones were forbidden to her under threat of dismissal.

Because it was restricted and therefore desirable, Selina yearned to sample the soft fruit of a ripe dream. Moving down the rows, she selected a dozen fruits, Old Punca's ration for each day. Selina selected the reddest, but a few had a purple tinge to them. Old Punca would save them for the end of the day when they fully ripened.

Selina sought to discover Old Punca's magical secrets by eavesdropping, but the woman's mutterings were unintelligible, and her spell books were written in an archaic language Selina couldn't read. She suspected the fruit provided Old Punca with pleasant dreams and gave her magical powers that extended her life.

As Selina turned to go, a ripe fruit dropped from the tree behind her. Old Punca didn't eat dream fruit which had been on the ground, but Selina picked it up. The fruit's deep red skin had split and revealed the rose-pink flesh inside. Juice dripped from the fruit onto Selina's fingers. Without thinking, she stuck two fingers in her mouth.

The garden disappeared, and she stood in an open courtyard. A carriage approached; the coachman dressed in dark green. Two black horses stopped and stamped the ground.

The prince, a handsome young man in a crown and wearing green that matched the carriage, jumped down and bowed to her. "Good evening, Princess. Are you ready for the ball?"

She looked at her pale blue gown encrusted with diamonds and embroidered rosebuds, fancier than anything she'd ever imagined. "Y-Yes." She took his arm, and he escorted her down the stairs to the carriage. She wasn't sure what was happening.

The carriage interior was dark, too dark. When a shadowy curtain fell away from her eyes, she found herself back in the garden dressed in homespun. She stared at the bruised fruit in her hand before dropping it and wiping her hand on her apron. A handsome prince? She'd been inside someone's dream! Probably that of a serving wench like herself. She had a ballgown dream occasionally, but never one so real.

No wonder Old Punca smiled at empty air all day. Selina covered the damaged fruit with leaves and returned to the cottage, locking the gate behind her.

She washed the fruits with fresh well water. As she gently dried the day's harvest, Selina recalled the honey sweetness she'd tasted, and the dreams held inside the fruit. Loving families? Rich food and good friends? She'd settle for a night with the handsome, green-garbed prince. She placed the fresh fruit in a bowl and set it beside the old woman's chair. Clearing the breakfast bowls, gently so as not to wake the old woman from her nap, Selina's cheeks flushed with the injustice of being so close to the fruit and not being allowed to taste it.

Old Punca was frail. Tipping the old woman's chair over backward might break her thin neck and leave the garden of dream fruit for Selina. No one would know.

She returned to the kitchen to cook lunch, contemplating

Old Punca having a deadly accident. Who would care if the old woman died? She had no friends or relatives. No one would miss her.

Selina selected a big knife and slipped behind Old Punca, now awake and nibbling the ripe fruit Selina had gathered. Thinking only of the garden and the wonderful dreams within her grasp, Selina stabbed the old woman in the back. Punca sputtered and choked before falling forward out of the chair.

A sharp blow stung her cheek. Selina found herself lying in the garden with Old Punca standing over her. Selina had dreamt she'd stabbed her mistress.

"You stupid girl!" Old Punca's eyes blazed with anger. "I warned you not to taste the dream fruit. You see your heart's desire, but you'll be forever trapped in a dream."

Selina stood in the garden. A half-eaten fruit lay on the ground beside her. She held her sticky fingers away from her beautiful gown as Punca hobbled out of the garden.

A royal coach pulled up outside the gate.

# THE GIFT OF MUSIC

## Michael Haynes

Jennifer hefted the last of her thirteenth birthday presents—a large box, shipped from her father stationed overseas.

"Do you know what it is?" she asked her mother.

Jennifer's mom, kneeling on the floor to clean up the mess Alan—one of the toddlers she babysat—had made of his lunch, shook her head. "He didn't tell me, love."

Jennifer peeled the wrapping off slowly as yet another ad for New Coke started on TV. The box beneath was plain; nearly half the paper was off before the word "RADIO" showed.

Despite herself, Jennifer frowned a bit as she pulled the radio from its styrofoam packing.

"Something wrong?" her mother asked.

She'd hoped maybe it would have been a CD player; Michelle had just gotten one for her thirteenth birthday. But this didn't even have a tape deck and was way too big to be portable. She swallowed her disappointment, forced a smile.

"No, Mom. It's just kinda heavy. Trying to think of a safe place for it."

In fact, it fit perfectly at the top of the bookshelf in her room, one of the sturdiest pieces of furniture they owned since it bore the weight of her many books. She plugged the radio in and twisted the dial to 103.7, her favorite station. Only static greeted her. She bit her lip and tried her second favorite next. Nothing there either.

"Maybe there's an antenna?" Jennifer's mother said, feeling around the back of the radio.

From his play yard, Alan began to cry. Jennifer's mother sighed. "We'll figure it out, I promise."

Jennifer played with the dial, trying every station she could think of before finally going click by click through every single frequency. A tear leaked out of one eye as she reached the 88s.

She turned the dial to its last setting, 87.9. The room filled with music. Not just any music, but one of her favorite songs, "Walking on Sunshine." Her tears flowed freely now, relief and happiness blending with and almost obscuring the constant sense of missing someone she felt while her dad was away. She danced around the room, eyes closed, soaking in the music.

———

Even though the radio only picked up the one station (and thank goodness it wasn't an opera station, or worse, talk radio), its music was a regular companion for Jennifer through the rest of eighth grade and the following summer. A few times she'd tried to get 87.9 to come in on the car radio while her mom was driving, but she always got static there.

On her first day of ninth grade, she went downstairs for breakfast to a silent house. She'd known her mother wouldn't be there; her new job had her out the door at six most mornings. But this was a big day and she could've used a hug, or even a smile. Her stomach flipped and flopped through the Wheaties she poured herself from a box with Mary Lou Retton on the front.

"I can do this," she said back in her bedroom, dressing in the clothes she'd picked out for the day. Her mind and insides weren't so sure.

With ten minutes before she had to leave, Jennifer flipped on the radio. There was a moment of static and her heart sank even lower, but the piano intro to "I Will Survive" burst through the speaker. Jennifer closed her eyes and swayed, singing along, feeling her anxiety melt away.

"I can do this," she said as the song ended. And this time the rest of her body agreed.

———◆———

The Saturday morning after Homecoming, Jennifer slept in late. When she woke, sunlight filled her room and the clock showed almost noon. She wandered into the kitchen but stopped abruptly seeing her mother sitting at the table, head in her hands.

"Mom?"

Jennifer's mom looked up, eyes red, face coated in tears. Jennifer's throat tightened.

"Mom? What's going on?"

"Sit down."

Jennifer sat, mind racing, hoping maybe she hadn't woken up yet and that this was a nightmare.

"It's about your father..."

The other words washed over Jennifer, and she screamed and cried and bolted from the chair. She ran to her room and locked the door. There she huddled on the floor as deep sobs racked her body.

Eventually Jennifer cried herself out. She was thirsty and achy. But when she stood, the first thing she did was turn on her radio.

Her knees went weak and she grabbed on to the bookshelf. "Lean on Me," a song her father had sung to soothe her so many times when she was a little girl and had skinned her knees or been teased by a playmate or suffered any of the other hurts of childhood, was playing.

The song ended. And then it began again. And again.

Jennifer swallowed hard and straightened up. She stroked the top of the radio.

"Thanks, Dad."

# WINGING IT

## *Magnolia Silcox*

Our world has always been shrouded in magic and mystery. We were all told tales of these powerful women that helped turn women into princesses. Ever since I was a little boy, I enjoyed sewing gorgeous dresses, hats, and shoes for women. I have always had big dreams of becoming a fashion designer. Of becoming a fairy godmother or godfather. Yet my father has always brushed it off as a childish dream.

"Callum, the men of our family have always been glassblowers and will always be glassblowers. I just don't see your little hobby going anywhere." he sighed.

Perhaps he was right. Besides, fairy godmothers were all these gorgeous magical women, and I was just a greasy commoner man at that. I had no use for such daydreamy idleness. That was until an unusual stranger came to my shop one day.

"Callum, this unusual mademoiselle would like to see you!" my father shouted.

When I went to the front of the store, I dropped my hammer at the sight of this mystical being. She had large dark blue wings and long blue hair. Her skin was a rosy pink, and her dress was made entirely out of flowers. I had never seen a fairy before, and they were just as beautiful as I had imagined.

"Pleasure to meet you miss, my name is Callum." I announced.

"Miss Patricia Presto is my name. I believe you'd be the perfect fairy godmother," she stated.

I began jumping up and down exhilarated by the prospect. My dreams were finally coming true. As for my father I could see sadness in his eyes as he bid me farewell. We didn't know when we'd cross paths again.

"Callum Carver, I was wondering if you'd like to accept an apprenticeship from me as a fairy-godmother-in-training. In New Calindria, I saw your girlfriend Miss Jessie Fordham wearing the most exquisite cyan ball gown. She said that you were the creator." Patricia explained.

"Yes!" I exclaimed.

Patricia took my hand and walked with me out the door. I said goodbye to Father and Patricia swirled her wand, creating a gold sparkly dust. With that, I was flying through the desert like a bird. We were up so high in the air that the pink glowing mountains looked like tiny jagged triangles. Up through the airy clouds we went, until we came across a castle in the sky. I had never seen a more brilliant building before. The castle was painted with all the colors of a sunrise in the sky. The hues of light pink, orange, yellow, and purple. Through the castle, we entered a prism-shining office.

"Now then Callum, to become a true fairy godmother you must earn your wings. Now I'll send you on your merry way to Summerset, New Calindria to help a lady in need called Ella. She is in a rather nasty predicament." Patricia stated.

With a poof of her fairy wand, I appeared in front of a heartbroken Miss Ella. Her dress was all tattered and torn into smithereens beyond repair and she was bawling her eyes out. Shards of sharp broken pieces of glass littered the floor. She looked up at me all teary-eyed and dried her sniveling.

"Who are you? Are you here to tear up my dress even more? My stepsisters already finished the job for you with those pieces of mirror glass." she cried.

"I am your fairy godmother, Callum," I replied.

"Really? I've never heard of a guy fairy godmother. Aren't you supposed to look fancy? You're all covered in dust and grime like when I clean the chimney in wintertime. My sisters Tammy and Tara mock me and call me Cinder Ella because I'm always covered in cinders by the time I'm done." Ella exclaimed.

This was my chance to prove to myself that if I could make something out of nothing then not only her wishes could come true but mine as well.

"Gather your things and let's go," I stated.

Ella then ran up to her room and changed into a ratty old dress and shoes. I stayed behind and collected the shards of glass and white silk fabric. What was I supposed to do with this mess? Patricia then came and escorted Ella and me away to her office. Ella waited out in the lobby while I got started designing. I would use the silk pieces, hemming them together to make a bodice. Patricia found me some sparkly white lace and so I used this trim to create ruffles and frills. But what was I to do with the glass shards? I pondered for a while on what to do until I finally decided. I could blow torch the pieces together to create a pair of shoes. Hours on end I spent melting the glass down into a ball. Then, I took two pieces and molded them into clear glass shoes.

After Patricia used her wand to transform my dress into reality. Miss Ella was fitted into the beautiful gown in a dressing room filled with other fairies. Ella came out of the dressing room elated with the biggest grin on her face. She wrapped her arms around me and hugged me as tightly as she could.

"I love it, Callum! You are truly the best fairy godfather ever." Ella beamed.

" Ella, you're the one who inspired me. You truly are the best princess ever," I admitted.

"Not yet he isn't. Mr. Callum Carver, I now pronounce you the first fairy godfather." Patricia stated.

With that, she waved her rainbow wand, and then white glittery sparkles began to cover my body. Translucent glass-like wings covered my back. My old greasy shop clothes turned into a silky white suit, and I had a glass wand. I couldn't fathom something like this happening in my wildest of dreams. That small boy in his father's glassblowing shop was now a fabulous fairy. I can finally tell him: Congrats, kid. We finally made it.

# THE LONELY PRINCESS

## *Dawn DeBraal*

Princess Gwendolyn walked out into the forest daily to sing to the birds. Her beautiful voice rang through the trees, and the birds sang back to her. A magpie even tried to copy her tune. She was lonely in the world. The king forbade her to leave the castle property, for there were marauders and evil-doers afoot. Until the uprising was put down with the help of her prince, the princess had to be very careful.

The guard who followed her everywhere was discreetly tucked behind a tree. She wanted to catch a bird and bring it back with her to listen to its tune all day.

She sang, and a little bird perched on a branch near her. The tiny wren then sang with all of his heart. Gwendolyn used her operatic voice to trill; the wren sang his sweet song back.

She held her hand to the little bird, but the wren flew away. Disappointed, she left the woods and trudged back to the castle. She would charm that little wren out of the trees. She was sure of it.

Gwendolyn returned to the woods the following morning and sang sweetly and the birds responded. The little wren sat on a branch near her and matched her voice until a mangy cat came out of the woods and scared the bird away.

"Look what you've done!" She shook her finger at the cat, who pushed himself against her legs. "You are getting my dress dirty; go away," Gwendolyn shouted, brushing the cat away. She ran back to the castle, upset. She had gotten so close to the wren she almost had him until that mangy cat came.

Sitting out in the gardens, she spied the cat again, slinking along the stone wall, watching her from a distance. She wondered what the cat's story was. It wasn't a palace cat, for if it were, he would be well fed, and his coat would be shiny.

She left him lying in the sun in the far distance and found the guard who watched over her.

"Do you see that cat over there? Do you know where he came from?"

"No, Princess, I only saw him yesterday when he approached you in the woods and again today."

"Thank you, Templin." Gwendolyn went about doing princess things, blessing the crops, and giving awards to citizens who had done wonderful things when her guard Templin approached her.

"Your Highness, Prince Caul has been listed as missing." Gwendolyn clutched her heart. Her fiance, Caul, was supposed to return from the front line any day."

"What do you mean missing?"

"He disappeared sometime last week, but they haven't found a body. That could mean he is alive and might have been captured. No one knows." Gwendolyn thanked the

160

guard and walked into the woods with Templin quietly following her.

She sat down and cried for her handsome prince. The wren came near and sang to her. Through teary eyes, she looked up at him and thanked the bird for his gift. Gwendolyn held her hand up, and the little wren landed on her finger. She gently placed her other hand over the top of him. She had captured the little wren.

Gwendolyn ran back to the castle, put the little wren in a gilded cage and hung him in the window. She would have his song with her all day long.

The wren either sat quietly or hung on the side of the cage beating his wings and trying to escape.

"Little bird, sing to me." Gwendolyn sang to him. He sat quietly and did not return the song. Gwendolyn took the cage outside the following day and sang to the little bird, who did not respond.

"Why won't you sing, little bird?" she asked the wren.

"Princess, he will not sing because he is not happy," Templin told her. Gwendolyn looked at the bird in the cage and wept. She felt terrible for stealing the birds' freedom so she took him back to the forest and opened the cage. The little wren flew into a tree.

The Princess sang her song, and the bird responded. It brought tears to her eyes, she had no right to capture the wren and hold him in a cage, but Gwendolyn was still sad.

The mangy cat came up to her, rubbing himself on her legs. Gwendolyn sighed and reached down to pet the sorry-looking cat. He purred in her arms, a joyful sound in her sadness.

"Oh, poor thing, you may come home with me and catch

mice in the castle." She returned to the castle and gave the cat to one of the servants.

"Please give him a scrubbing, and when he is dry, bring him to my quarters." The servant curtsied. An hour later, a light tapping on the door to the princess's room.

"Enter," she commanded, and the maid walked in with a beautiful fluffy cat. She put the cat on the floor and closed the door behind her.

"My, aren't you the handsome cat." Gwendolyn patted the bed, and the cat jumped up, allowing her to scratch his chin. His purring grew louder. "Oh, kitty, I am so lonely. The enemy has captured Prince Caul; I am afraid I will never see him again." Tears flowed from her eyes when the cat came and sat in her lap. Gwendolyn hugged the stray cat and kissed his head.

The cat jumped out of her lap, meowing loudly and circling when he transformed into Prince Caul.

"My beloved!" Gwendolyn raced into Prince Caul's arms.

"Thank you, Gwendolyn. A witch turned me into a cat to escape my captors; I had to get you to kiss me for the spell to be broken."

The little wren landed in a tree outside her window and sang his heart out as the lovers embraced. The princess was no longer lonely.

# Hand Me Down My Walking Shoes

## *Maureen Bowden*

Angie's grandson pushed her, in her wheelchair, into the garden. "Here you are, Gran," he said. "Your favourite spot."

"Thanks, pet," she said. "You toddle off now. I'll be fine here for an hour or so." She was content, sitting close to her stone Buddha that rested in a leafy alcove upon a slab of recycled slate. Wide, fresh hydrangea leaves caressed his shoulder, their flat surfaces finely veined, and their stems swaying in the late morning breeze.

She closed her eyes and waited for the god Morpheus to appear, as he always did, in the guise of a lost loved one, of which there were many, and the numbers were growing. Morpheus was the kind friend who brought them back.

Footsteps alerted her to the young man striding across the lawn. She laughed. He was just as she remembered: not a day over nineteen, cock o' the walk, acting as if he owned the place, long, multi-pocketed parka, dark wavy hair and a sexy smile. Oliver Dennison. "Hello, Denny," she said. "It's been quite a while."

She remembered walking hand in hand with him through the city backstreets on a warm summer night many years ago. She'd been wearing new shoes and they hurt her feet. They'd stopped for a rest outside Saint Luke's, the shell of a church that had been bombed in the Blitz and left standing as a war memorial. The roofless interior had been invaded by vegetation. Through the empty window recesses it looked like an alien jungle. The place gave her the creeps. She'd had nightmares about it as a child. She shivered. Denny took off his parka and draped it around her shoulders. They sat and leaned against the church wall. She kicked off her shoes, blue plastic with ankle straps and square heels. They'd be great for dancing once she'd broken them in. He picked them up and tucked them close to the wall. "Leave them here. Nobody's gonna see them. I'll come back and get them tomorrow." He massaged her ankles, and she wriggled her toes in pleasure. The pavement felt cool on the soles of her bare feet as they made their way home.

He told her that when he went back for the shoes they'd gone. She wasn't sure she believed he went back for them. He promised to buy her another pair, but he didn't.

On their last day together they strolled through the city to the Pierhead and sat by the river sharing an orange. "I want to see the world, Angie," he said. The city couldn't hold him and neither could she.

A month later he was in Israel working in a Kibbutz. She had no idea where he went after that. Now Morpheus had brought him back to her. "I missed you." She said.

"But you soon forgot me. When I came back for the first time you were a married lady with babies and a mortgage."

"I had my own life to lead."

"Did you find the life you wanted?"

"Yes, did you?"

He shrugged. "I was never sure what I wanted."

"How did you die, Denny?"

"I fell into the Orinoco."

She knew he'd lie. A mutual friend had posted the truth on Facebook. His heart and liver finally gave up the struggle against the effects of rough living and copious amounts of alcohol. He died a lonely death, but the Orinoco had a better ring to it.

"You should have been more careful, but you were right to leave. You made a lot of memories for yourself and in the end that's all we have."

"You could have come with me, Angie. I asked you to. Remember?"

She shook her head. "No, I don't remember you asking, but I wouldn't have gone with you anyway"

"Why not?"

"Because I wanted to be a married lady with babies and a mortgage."

"Well, come with me now."

"Where would we go?"

"Into the Beyond, to see what's there."

"But I can't walk."

"Yes, you can. It's time. I'll help you."

She pulled back the blanket that covered her knees and

looked at her feet, encased in the Spiderman slipper-socks that were a birthday present from her youngest granddaughter. "I don't have shoes."

"Oh, sorry. I forgot." He plunged his hand into the deepest pocket of his parka and pulled out her blue plastic shoes with ankle straps and square heels. "They're not new anymore, so they won't hurt you." He removed her slipper socks and fitted the shoes onto her feet.

She looked into his face. He was no longer Denny, but everyone she'd loved and lost. She saw her adored granddad, her mother and father, favourite aunts and uncles, childhood pals, companions of her teenage days, work mates, lovers and friends, and her husband: her children's father, the love of her life. They called to her. They were waiting for her. She stepped into the garden. Morpheus took her hand and led her into the Beyond.

# GORGE

## *L.N. Hunter*

One hundred and thirty-seven bowls of finest Beluga caviar had been arranged on the deep red tablecloth. On the next table were ninety-six dishes of exquisite Sicilian lobster bisque. After that came eighty-three plates of Kobe rib-eye, pale squiggles of Venezuelan horseradish glaze tracing identical paths across the plates. Dessert was caramelized apricot, glistening in one hundred and fifty-nine Japanese porcelain bulbs. The final table in this part of the room offered twelve cheese boards, draped with a fine embroidered muslin cloth to prevent their rich odors from overpowering the mouth-watering aromas of the other courses. At the other end of the room, more tables strained under similar quantities of *foie gras*, fugu slivers in Vietnamese noodle soup, roast guinea fowl with shredded vegetables, hand-etched bowls of Parisian *chocolat noir*, and another mountain of rare cheeses.

A fanfare of trumpets announced the arrival of the audience. On one side was Prince Rathbone of Erigonia, with his retinue of sycophants. On the other, Duke Ferdinand of Alutriea, accompanied by his entourage of fawning toadies. Today's contest would decide who would rule the combined country.

Another fanfare sounded, and two people lumbered in to polite applause. They were big people, huge people, enormously wide and tall, massively muscled, grim-faced giants.

Before taking up his position in the middle of the room, Alphonse Patique, dark-haired and dark-eyed, bowed—as much as the mountain of a man was able—to his patron Duke Ferdinand, who returned a cruel-lipped smile. Flaxen-haired Ingrid von Scherwand stood beside Alphonse, and similarly acknowledged Prince Rathbone.

The adjudicator gave the signal, and the contenders launched themselves at their respective tables.

Alphonse attacked the truffles, each bowlful disappearing in a single gulp. Ingrid inhaled her foie gras. They ignored the spoons for the second course and poured the bisque and noodle soups into the vast tunnels of their throats. Barely slowing, they tackled their third tables, shoveling prime steak and guinea fowl into their mouths, not taking time to chew, instead guzzling down whole cuts.

If Ingrid and Alphonse had been able to spare a glance for their audience, all they would have seen was a seething mass of sweaty red faces, cheering and jeering at the contestants in equal measure.

Alphonse had been very young when he was chosen as a competitive eater. His initial pride at being selected quickly dissolved into misery. From the start, he was force-fed dry sweetened flour, followed by liters of water to cause it to swell and stretch his stomach. His taste buds were subjected to caustic liquids, so the hottest chilies and coldest ices wouldn't slow his gorging. He endured exhausting jaw exercises to ensure he could bite through the hardest of crusts, and the fitting of painful throat-widening devices to facilitate the flow of bulky items, meant to reduce chewing time. Training was not all about the alimentary canal: strong arms and powerful, grasping hands were required to propel the food into his gaping mouth, and sturdy legs to lurch across tables, hurling his body from one dish to the next.

When Ingrid and Alphonse finished the dessert table—at practically the same time—they both simply stopped. They nodded once at each other, then turned towards their audience and profusely vomited over them. Slimy beef and fowl, mashed vegetable chunks, and foul-smelling, acid-drenched seafood splattered clothes and floor.

The horrified nobles fled, abandoning the two royals and their personal guards. Swords and arrows had little effect on Ingrid's and Alphonse's bulk—equal measures of rock-hard muscle and sensation-free fat—and the unstoppable pair remorselessly bulldozed and incapacitated the guards.

The gorgers dragged the deserted royals to the middle of the floor and sat on them. Prince Rathbone lost his ability to protest as Alphonse rested his bulk upon him, and he finally expired with a feeble crunch. Duke Ferdinand emitted a last deflating exhalation from underneath Ingrid.

A few days later, the alliance of Erigonia and Alutriea was sealed with the marriage of Ingrid and Alphonse, an occasion marked by another huge feast of fine food. This time, however, the tables were all but ignored by the new husband and wife, who had eyes only for each other.

# What You Needed

## *Christopher J. Burke*

Julian's eyes blinked open for half a second. He became aware of the ground beneath him, and the grass that he was lying upon. When he opened his eyes again, what he thought had been gray skies were bright blue. He didn't feel alive, but all indications pointed to it being so. He had no idea where he was.

"Sit up whenever you're ready," a voice called to him. "But you may want to take it slowly. Everyone rushes to their feet, and then they wish they hadn't."

Turning his head to the right, Julian saw a middle-aged woman, with some gray mixed in with her brown hair and wearing glasses. She was standing perpendicular to his field of vision. He sat up to see her standing in a dirt road.

"That's right. Give it a minute before you stand."

Julian jumped to his feet and immediately regretted the decision. He wasn't light-headed but his thoughts were clouded. He had a hard time forming a coherent thought. Raising a hand above his eyes, Julian turned in place and took in the view. The countryside was filled with trees and wildflowers and a few dirt roads. He didn't spot any houses, barns, or farms. Not even a gas station or a Starbucks.

He looked to the strange woman. "I'm sorry. But I don't seem to know where I am or how I got here. It looks like I'm in a park in Pennsylvania or Ohio or...someplace. But that's not possible."

The woman laughed. "Oh, you'd be surprised what's possible. It's a lovely place though, isn't it?"

"What is this place?"

"Oh, I wouldn't know. I've never seen it before."

Julian stepped out of the grass and down onto the road. He approached the woman with caution, not that he thought she'd pull a knife from her shoulder bag. "I don't understand. You don't know where we are, either?"

The woman smiled. "Generally, yes, but this not-place we're standing in; it's here because you needed it."

"Because I needed it?"

She shifted her bag to her other shoulder. "Yes. When you first opened your eyes, what did you see?"

"Nothing. Just gray."

"And the second time, the sky was blue. Because that's what you needed it to be. It helps your mind cope as your soul adjusts."

Julian stopped in his tracks. "My soul? I'm –?"

"Dead," she completed.

"And you're an angel?"

Another laugh erupted. "Oh, Heavens, no. I'm another soul like you. You can call me Lucy. Consider me your afterlife welcoming committee."

She offered her hand, and Julian hesitated to take it. Since he wasn't thinking clearly, he wanted to go with his gut, but his insides weren't telling him anything. *Because I'm dead*, he thought. He kicked a stone and watched it skip away. It felt real enough, but it still seemed wrong.

Julian held his arms out. "But why are you welcoming me on a dirt road in the middle of nowhere?"

Lucy shrugged. "We're not nowhere. We're just between places. Maybe you needed to take a walk and feel the fresh air. It'll clear your head."

His head did need clearing. "What if I said I needed an Uber to come by and give us a ride?"

The woman stopped to consider that. "Let's see." She turned and looked down the road. Julian did the same and stared into the distance to the point where the road disappeared over a small rise. No clouds of dust kicked up.

After a few minutes, Lucy turned back. "I guess you didn't need that. Shall we go? We should make it by sundown."

Until that moment, Julian hadn't been aware of the sun. But now he could see it in the sky, and he noticed the shadows at their feet trailing behind them. "Where are we going?"

She touched his shoulder. "You'll know it when you see it."

Julian nodded. "I know, because it'll be what I need. But how do I know what I need? I'm here for eternity. What do I do with myself?"

Lucy reached into her bag and pulled out some brochures. "Well, besides the usual meditation, reflection and choir practice, there are a lot of activities to try. Mountain climbing, baking, restoring classic cars... Do you like to fish? As you might guess we have a lot of fishers up here."

Julian grunted. "I didn't really have any hobbies, and I didn't think I'd need to find one to occupy myself."

"Oh, dear." She stuffed everything back into her bag. "There's literally an infinite number of things to try. And nearly infinite time to do it all."

"Am I in Hell?"

Lucy gasped.

Julian stared right into her eyes, the windows to her soul. "Because Heaven doesn't seem to be the place I thought it would be." He kicked another rock. This one bounced four times and then plinked off something metal.

The pair turned their heads to where the sound had come. There was an aluminum can lying in the grass next to the road.

"Seriously?" A loud puff of air escaped Julian's lips. "There's a trash problem in Heaven? You can't keep the roads clean in the afterlife? Bad enough that we had to put up with it on Earth. Did some yahoo in a pickup truck just throw his empty out the window as he rumbled on by? Is this something you need?"

A scowl crossed Lucy's face. "I told you. This place was created for you."

Julian stomped down the road and glared at the can.

Lucy came up beside him. Her scowl vanished. She was smiling. "Do you need to get that?"

Instinct took over. Julian bent down and retrieved the can. "Why would I need this?"

Lucy patted Julian's chest over his heart. "Because being of service is what your soul needs. That's the greatest hobby you could have. You're going to be very happy here."

# LUCKY

## *Helen Liptak*

The orange flash distracts me from my workout. Ugh! Not again! I slow the exercise bike, searching past therapists and patients. Where'd it go? Did I imagine it? I thought the exorcism worked and I'd never see them again.

One offhand remark last year in Ireland attracted a brogue-speaking, shamrock-loving entity, and the creatures have been pestering me ever since. How was I to know calling them *Lucky* was rude? That didn't give them the right to take over my life. Now it's impossible to get rid of them, even convince anyone else to acknowledge them. I only started trapping them when they kept interfering, ruining relationships and my reputation. I really thought I ended it last time.

But they're back.

I double down on the pedals, pushing my limits, working off my frustration. They follow me everywhere, but no one else sees them or believes in them. Apparently, that's all they need to threaten my sanity and my health. A twinge from the last injury they caused reminds me to slow down and act rationally.

Just as I begin to hope I'd imagined this latest sighting, I spot one of the red-headed rascals peeking over the shoulder of a baseball player with a torn rotator cuff. It ducks behind the guy's head and I drop my eyes. Can't let it see it got to me. I pretend to check the read-out for my vitals. Huh. Five minutes to go and already 100 calories burned. At least the supernatural infestation has some benefits.

I keep my head down and blow a lock of hair off my face, fuming and planning. Leprechauns are supposed to be elusive, solitary creatures, invisible even when people who believe that pot of gold at the end of the rainbow malarkey search for them. Idiots! Everyone knows magical beings aren't benevolent. I'm living proof every magical gift has strings attached like fairy tales warn. I should've paid better attention.

There it goes again! Without moving my head, I track the red hair and traditional red coat. He's not some green-coated TV ad version, or even the horror movie one. He's another too clever pain-in-my-butt pest, specializing in everyday annoyances like wobbly shopping cart wheels or sand in your shoes or ear worms. The Wee Folk excel at those. Why do exciting things like banshees foreshadowing death or kelpies drowning riders when you can deliver annoying mood swings, accidents, and depression? No one connects that to meddling remnants of old legends. Except me, and I wish I didn't. I'd rather be cluelessly depressed like the rest of humanity, not recognize the leprechaun responsible. Maybe that's why they pick on me. I'm the only one onto them, no matter who I try to convince otherwise.

The baseball player scowls. He must feel the unseen

pest sinking claws into his calf, working its way toward his thousand-dollar shoes even if he can't see it. Why do I have to? I can't ignore it even if acknowledging it will transfer its mischief to me. But if I don't do something expensive athletic shoeswill mysteriously self-destruct followed by more disasters. My conscience won't let the imp harass this guy and make his life miserable. I sigh. They rely on being invisible so one hard stare sends 'Lucky' scuttling away from his target. For now.

They love shoes. And gold. I trapped one using an heirloom emerald ring. I guess releasing it with a stern warning instead of cashing in on its gifts was insulting. And a sign of weakness. Never mind I don't want its treasures or anything to do with them. Ever. That triggered some kind of vendetta and now I'm a leprechaun magnet, someone to practice pranks on. One of them caused this latest injury, but try telling that to doctors. Disbelief guarantees their invisibility and invisibility guarantees disbelief.

At first I was charmed by them. Freaked out, but charmed. I felt privileged to meet one of the notoriously skittish Wee Folk. Until their mischief accelerated. Now no shoes are safe, my best whiskey disappears, and my life is in shambles. I captured the original culprit and wished him away without using up all the available wishes which encouraged another one to try his luck. I didn't figure that out for a while.

I never even asked about their gold. Big mistake. That only convinced them I was a pushover, and more wizened, pipe-smoking, miniature cobblers came out of the woodwork to drive me crazy. Last time I nabbed one, I tried the exorcism. It's been blessedly quiet ever since. Until this one.

I finish my workout session, gulp my water, and gather my things as glittering eyes and a sly smile creep toward my shoe. No one else notices. If they did, maybe that'd end the curse. Ignoring the sneak until he's within arm's reach, I snatch him up by his coattails, coughing loudly to cover his outraged squawks.

No more playing nice.

This time I'll keep eyes on the belligerent little beast until it promises immunity from supernatural visits. Stuffing him into my athletic bag, I wave to the physical therapists, pretend to search through my satchel, and limp out. I narrow my eyes, warning it. It has the audacity to flash its supposedly charming grin at me from the depths of the bag.

"All three wishes, your gold, and immunity!" I hiss, without breaking eye contact. I stay focused and step into the parking lot, determined to break the curse.

Brakes squeal. There's a thud, an irritating laugh, then darkness.

"Why'd you walk right in front of me, lady?" The voice of a UPS driver hoisting me onto the curb penetrates my consciousness. "What was that thing?"

"You saw him?" Hope overrides my pain.

He nods, confused. "Yes!"

I smile at this poor, unsuspecting guy, pity struggling with relief.

From across the lot my tormenter shoots me an angry glare and howls in frustration.

The jig is up. He's been seen.

# A THOUSAND WORDS

## *Dawn Colclasure*

"You know she's not real, right?"

Andrew Mertz stared at the picture. All he could see was the woman smiling back at him. Sherry. Her name was Sherry. She was so beautiful. The way her chestnut hair fell to her shoulders, how the sun seemed to make her perfect skin shine and how her blue eyes sparkled as she smiled back at him.

"Andrew?"

He looked up and slumped back into his seat at the sight of his mother staring at him. She'd lost interest in the baked chicken and green beans he had cooked for her this evening. All she had done was complain about how bland the food tasted. He had hoped to find escape in Sherry's picture.

His mother's cold stare bore right into his soul.

"That is just a picture of a woman," she said. "You don't have the real thing in your life."

"I don't need the real thing," he muttered defiantly. "What I have with her is enough."

His mother rolled her eyes and sighed. "What you have with

179

her is a fantasy. I don't know why you stopped trying to find someone new after things ended with your latest girlfriend. You are 32 years old. Honestly, how hard can it be for someone as handsome as you to find the right girl?"

"I have found the right girl," Andrew said. He smiled at the picture again. "Sherry. Sherry loves me. What we have is better than what I ever had with any other girl."

His mother sighed again and launched into another lecture about how Andrew should stop indulging in fantasy and find himself a real woman.

But Andrew wasn't listening. He was too busy staring at the picture of Sherry and smiling. And remembering his dream.

———

She smiled as she took his hand. Her skin was so soft. Her smile made him feel like everything was right with the world, just like it always did.

"I will always love you," she said, with that angelic voice she had. "No matter what happens."

She leaned forward to kiss him and he took her into his arms. The kiss deepened. Soon they were in bed together, making love. Andrew actually felt her touching him and he felt himself climax.

Their lovemaking was so intense that he woke from his dream.

He breathed heavily as he sat up in bed, waiting as the feelings of ecstasy faded from him and his body stopped shuddering from pleasure.

He'd had another dream of her. And just like the last dream, it had been exactly the same as what he had written. The exact same fantasy of what he had written in his diary the day before.

Andrew groaned as he lay back down in bed. He stiffened, hoping the sound didn't wake his mother. She probably couldn't hear him, but she was such a light sleeper that he'd rather not take the chance.

He turned to look at the framed picture of Sherry that he kept on his nightstand. He grabbed it and held it tightly in front of his face. "I'll always love you too," he whispered. He clutched the picture to his chest, turning onto his side in his bed. "No matter what happens."

He was unable to fall back asleep but a smile formed on his face when he closed his eyes and started to fantasize about the woman in the picture.

———

"Andrew! My feet hurt! Come rub them for me!"

"Yes, Mother," Andrew replied. He got up from the chair he'd been sitting in to watch TV and walked into his mother's room. She lay in bed still wearing only her nightgown. It was the afternoon but she was too sick and too sore to do anything like getting dressed. She refused his offers to help. Andrew tried to accept that his elderly mother just couldn't do the things she used to do, like cook meals or go places, but it wasn't easy.

At least Sherry could do those things, and more. So much more.

He smiled as he started thinking about her, holding his mother's feet in his hands. How she could cook such an amazing dinner and clean the house so perfectly. She was always ready and willing to go with him to the movies or even to play a game with him, anytime he wanted to. Like his mother used to do, but didn't do anymore.

"Andrew! You're hurting me!"

Andrew snapped out of his fantasy. "Oh! Sorry, Mother. I-I-I—"

He ran out of the room to his own bedroom.

"Where are you going? Andrew! I need to take my pill! Andrew!"

He ran into his room and grabbed the picture he kept by the nightstand. He lay on his stomach on his bed, staring at her. "Please be real," he whispered. "Please be real. Please be real."

He relaxed on the bed and soon fell asleep. She was in his dream again, giving him everything he wanted. She was everything he wanted her to be, and more.

The dream was so real this time. So life-like. Andrew let go of the real world that he lived in, wanting only to stay with the woman of his fantasies. He felt himself being drawn into the dream, body and soul. He held onto Sherry with every ounce of his being.

While dancing, their heads slowly moved together and they kissed. This time, it was the most perfect, realistic kiss of all.

Andrew smiled as he slept, even as his heart slowly stopped beating and he disappeared into the dream world forever.

That was how he was found days later, dead on his bed with a smile on his face.

His mother, however, was not found smiling. She never got the heart pill that she needed. Never had her screams for help to her son answered. She died shortly after he did, clutching her heart with tears in her eyes for the beloved son she knew she had lost.

# Bunnies of the Apocalypse

## Gregg Chamberlain

"There's no point in shouting or screaming for help," said Mr. Seltzer. "No one can hear you."

Little Kyrie stared, wide-eyed, as the kindly-looking old man reached into a battered top hat. His arm went in up past the elbow. He drew out a big, wickedly sharp-looking knife. Its shiny blade gleamed in the flickering candlelight.

Seeing the child's astonished look, Mr. Seltzer smiled. "A useful little gift from my patron," he said, twirling the hat around on a finger. "Imagine what the Dark Lord will give me in exchange for you."

He pointed with the tip of the knife at the chalk outline of a pentagram on the floor. "Now, be a good little sacrifice and step inside. Mind you don't smudge any of the lines. Else it will prove unpleasant for you, and I'll just redraw the pentagram anyway."

Kyrie took one reluctant step towards the pentagram.

Without warning, the child darted aside, at the same time leaping towards Mr. Seltzer. Grabbing at the hat, Kyrie snatched it from the surprised old man's grasp.

Landing a couple of child-sized paces away, Kyrie ran the short distance to the door at the other side of the room. It was locked. The child spun around, one hand automatically reaching inside the hat.

Seltzer smiled and scoffed. "What do you think you are going to do with my hat? Pull a rabbit out?"

Desperate and despairing, while the still-smiling Satanist sneered and watched, Kyrie fumbled around inside the hat. Eyes widened with sudden hope as big furry fingers gripped a child-sized hand.

Kyrie tugged and pulled ... a rabbit out of the hat. A six-foot-tall rabbit that stood balanced upright on its backward-kneed legs. The red-furred creature looked like a rabbit version of Conan the Barbarian, muscles bulging up and down its legs and arms. One almost-human hand still grasped Kyrie's while the rabbit's other hand took quick possession of the hat.

The man-sized rabbit winked an eye at Kyrie, then turned towards Mr. Seltzer, who was still holding his knife, but standing open-mouthed now with shock.

"G'day, mate," the rabbit said.

The Satanist blinked. "Good day, mate?"

A pink nose twitched in amusement. "You were expecting maybe 'What's up, doc?' or something?"

The strange creature let go of Kyrie's hand. "S'cuse us half a mo', little bit, 'kay?" A large paw pushed the child protectively to one side and behind the big rabbit.

It held up the top hat. "Oi!" it called into the mouth of the brim. "Shake a paw, you lot. We got a job to do and no mistake, alright?"

Turning the hat right side up and holding it high, the rabbit gave a couple of sharp raps against the flat top. Out the open bottom end tumbled one, two, three more rabbit creatures, equal in size to the first but all differing in appearance.

One was a grey-furred female, skinny to the point of emaciation. Legs like narrow knotted tree limbs supported an anorexic body all bumpy with the ribs sticking out. At the end of twig-thin arms, bony fingers snatched and grabbed at empty air. Sharp white buck teeth in the deathshead skull gleamed in the candlelight.

Another member of the trio had sickly-yellow, mange-ridden hair, with leprous-grey skin showing in patches where the fur had fallen out. Feverish yellow eyes turned their burning gaze on Mr. Seltzer. Without thinking, he took an instinctive step back, bringing up his knife. A scabrous nose wrinkled up in amused response.

The last one of the creatures stood tall and silent like a midnight-furred shadow. Cataract-white eyes stared at the Satanist, who quailed beneath their chill regard.

"Right then," said the blood-red rabbit. "Introductions are in order." A furry thumb jerked towards its broad chest. "I'm War."

Mr. Seltzer gaped. War continued speaking.

"This darlin' here is Famine. Wouldn't stand too close to her just now, mind. She's feelin' a mite peckish."

Famine's hungry eyes took their measure of Mr. Seltzer. Her sharp white teeth snapped.

"You might have guessed this ugly mug's Plague."

Fever-bright eyes stared. Rotting lips revealed a pair of blackened buck teeth. "Brrrraaaaiiiinnnnsssss?"

"Well, I guess we know now what's the disease choice for today, eh?" War indicated the remaining member of the quartet. "Big and Quiet here's Death, if you didn't already know. But his friends all call him Harvey."

Death's paw-like hands flexed. Bone-white sickle claws snicked out of the finger tips.

Mr. Seltzer took a quick step back into the pentagram. Bending down, he swiftly scratched several symbols inside each of the five angles.

Straightening, he said with smug satisfaction, "I don't know who or what you are, but you cannot harm me." He pointed the knife tip at the pentagram and its new additions. "Not now that I have protection."

War's ears twitched. He snorted. "That's where yer wrong, ya stupid drongo."

All four rabbit-creatures advanced as one on the quaking Satanist. War held up the top hat. "We're takin' you back with us for a little meet-an'-greet with yer boss. All in one piece, or in pieces. Your choice, yob."

Mr. Seltzer fell to his knees. The forgotten knife sagged in his fingers. "But," he gabbled, "but it's my hat. My hat! How could that child use my hat?"

"Tsk," answered War, spinning the hat around on one furry finger. "It's just a simple old trick, is all."

Crimson eyes narrowed as a scarlet harelip split in a buck-tooth grin. "Everyone knows. Tricks are for kids."

# WHO IS THE GIANT?

## *Rhys Hughes*

When I was asked the question, "Who is the giant?" I was unable to answer it with any certainty, but I knew that a giant had been predicted by a prophet long ago and I supposed that the time was drawing near for the giant to appear and smash our city into small fragments. I was told, "We don't know who he is, a most unfortunate consequence of the prophecy being so short on detail, but we are certain the appointed day of his arrival is coming soon, and we want to be prepared." And they looked at me beseechingly. I was the strongest man in the city, probably in the entire land, a potential hero waiting for his moment. How could I refuse them or refuse myself?

I said, "I will take measures now to protect the city from the giant before he turns up, and when he is here, I will be in a position to oppose him," and the nods of agreement and sighs of relief were numerous and sincere among those who had approached me. My duty was plain. I needed to become stronger than I already was, to train my body to a peak of perfection, and to do that it was necessary that I spend most of my time in the gymnasium. The authorities arranged for the facilities to be wholly mine and they made it a crime for anyone else to use them until the giant was neutralised. I lifted weights for many hours every day and my muscles expanded.

My progress was rapid, for I was already an athlete, a strongman, a purely physical exemplar. Whether I could defeat a giant in single combat even when I was in my prime was another question. I was unable to answer with confidence, though I always said, "I will do my best and I suppose it will be enough," and my words were taken as evidence that I had a humble attitude and did not wish to tempt fate. I was extremely powerful by this stage but still only a man and it was unclear how large the giant would be. "All we know is that he will appear and then we will be able to judge his size and capabilities," they always replied to my questions. "Please be patient."

And I *was* patient, and dedicated too, and my muscles became bigger than they had ever been. I was constantly encouraged by my neighbours and indeed all the citizens of my city. Free food and drink were pressed upon me. Because my efforts in the gymnasium were so strenuous, this nourishment was crucial, and my size kept increasing. One evening, after a very lengthy session with all the weights piled up together, I found that I no longer was able to fit through the door. My muscles were too large. "What should I do?" I cried when I discovered that despite my great strength, the walls of the gymnasium were too solid for me to break. I was trapped in the building.

"We must consider the matter," they told me, "and in

the meantime, having nothing else to do, we suggest you keep exercising." Then they went away in an orderly group, undoubtedly to discuss what action to take. I resumed my lifting of the weights and the gymnasium became my permanent home in the days that followed. I knew that if I stopped exercising, my muscles would shrink. Then I would be able to pass through the door again. But what if the giant was waiting for just such a moment? He might be a cunning giant. It was hardly sensible for me to deliberately weaken myself now, so I continued building my body until I was the strongest man who ever lived.

Finally, I became so strong and large that I occupied the room in a tight fit. I was unable to turn around. The gymnasium was like a coffin to me. I strained my muscles, but the walls and roof had been reinforced beyond even my abilities to crack them. I was a prisoner. It was then that the last delegation visited. Standing outside the door, they said, "The prophet predicted the coming of the giant. Nobody knows who that giant is, nor when he will arrive; so, we thought it best to get the unpleasant business over with and we chose you for the role." Then I knew that it was really I who was the giant. The danger was past, and with both regret and relief I wept in my trap.

# THE WISH

## *C Lenz*

Princess Ella glided through the carnival in her gilded litter. Four liveried servants carried her past dancers and jugglers, her guards maintaining a bulwark against the pointing, gawking crowd.

Through a veil of silk, the princess read the illustrated posters festooning the sideshow. *The Living Corpse*, one of them said. An old woman slept in a glass case below the sign, a mirror under her nose to show her steady breath. The crowd banged on the glass. She didn't stir.

Beside the glass coffin, golden hair trailed on the dusty ground, studded with debris from the well-trod dirt. The gilded strands looped and twisted in wide circles around a young woman in a simple dress. More of her tresses draped across her shoulder and over the poster calling her the Locked Maiden.

The last of the attractions was like a beacon on her dias. Her snow-white skin blazed bright in the glow from a nearby fire-eater. Painted letters on a banner proclaimed her the Parchment Girl. A cluster of passing men curled their lips in disgust, and a wide-eyed young woman held her arm up to the Parchment Girl's to goggle at the difference in their skin tone.

Ella frowned. It was as she had heard.

Her carriage shuddered. One of the servants had shied away from a man in a patchwork cloak, no two scraps the same color. "That's close enough," one of the guards growled, pressing a gauntlet to the man's chest.

Princess Ella lifted the curtain separating her from the world. The smell of hay and dung wafted through the cloud of potpourri perfuming her carriage.

"Move along," the guard commanded.

"No," Ella told him. She sat up, pushing layers of skirts aside. "I would speak to this man."

That was all the permission the rainbow harlequin needed to shove past the guard. "My lady, it is an honor," he said, bowing low in front of the Princess, almost sweeping the feather on his hat into the dirt. "I am Corso. Welcome to my carnival."

"It is quite a display," Ella observed.

"You don't approve?" Corso gasped, covering his goateed chin with a gloved hand. "Please, let me know how I can make you happy. It has been a long time since I've entertained nobility. What do you wish?"

Ella cocked her head. "Is it true that you've made that offer before?" she asked. She looked down the line of women being displayed for entertainment. "Let's see, she wished for sweet dreams, she wished for golden hair, and she wished for fair skin. Am I correct?"

Corso shrugged. "In their own way, they all wished to be undesirable."

"Indeed."

"Please, my Princess," Corso bowed again, staying bent in submission. "I only wish to serve. When each of them came to me, they were looking to escape however they could."

Ella watched the Parchment Girl lace her skeletal fingers with the soft pink hand of a little girl. Beside her, children shoved flowers into the Locked Maiden's endless cascade of hair. She wondered how long they'd be forced to stand there that day, smiling indulgently at staring strangers. At least the Living Corpse did not have to perform from inside her box.

"You took advantage of them," the Princess spat. "You twisted their words to mean whatever served you."

The showman's head jerked up, a glint in his eye. "And what about you? You knew this game and you sought me out anyway." He rose, slowly stretching to his full height. "What is it you wish to escape? An arranged marriage, perhaps?"

"No. Well, yes, but I don't want to escape. Unlike you, I don't wish to only serve myself." Ella set her jaw. She glared at Corso, hoping her eyes looked as hard as steel, even if her heart fluttered like a bird trapped in a cage. "Villains like you have no place in this realm. I wish to scour my kingdom clean."

Corso let out a high, cold laugh. He held up his right hand. An evil grin stretched across his face. "Your wish is my command." His fingers snapped like thunder.

Ella's hands were wet and warm. Wrinkled from the water. A dishcloth dropped from her fingers with a moist slap while a wooden bowl clattered to the ground.

The Princess stared at the strange room. The packed

dirt floor, the rough stone walls, the tin washing basins. She had never seen this place, but the windows showed views of pastures and fields that she recognized, albeit from much higher up. The breeze brought the smell of grass and manure. As she spun to take in her new surroundings, the rough burlap dress she wore rubbed against her skin.

"Ella!" a voice called. "Stop daydreaming!"

Ella snatched the bowl and dishcloth off the ground. "Yes, mistress," she called back to the cook. "Sorry, mistress."

For her whole life, Ella had been swathed in beautiful silks and furs, perfectly perfumed and coiffed. But it was all to present her as a pretty bauble to dangle before the masses. To parade her in front of audiences during ceremonies. Eventually, she would be wrapped in white lace and pearls and gifted to some nobleman's son. Her careless wish had been just as irresistible as she had hoped.

The Servant Girl smiled to herself as she went back to scrubbing the dishes.

# Cordelia's Conundrum

## *Shari Held*

Cordelia blinked back her tears. She only had twenty-four hours to retrieve the spell book from Nix, the goblin who'd stolen it. The spell book belonged to Juniper, the witch who ruled over the Emerald Forest where they all made their home.

Cordelia didn't know who scared her more—Nix or Juniper. Playing negotiator between those two was a sure way to get turned into a slug—or worse. But Cordelia had no choice if she wanted to see her sister Selwyn again.

Selwyn, who cleaned Juniper's castle, had let Nix in, not suspecting she intended to steal the spell book. Enraged, Juniper threatened to sell Selwyn if Cordelia didn't recover the book. Human-sized fairies fetched a high price in the Magical Marketplace, and Selwyn was one of the fairest of a species known for their beauty.

Solving a dispute between the witch and the goblin would require finesse and courage. Could she do it? She must. Selwyn's future depended on it.

Cordelia knew she'd increase her odds for success if she weren't so rattled. She rubbed her palms together, placed them against the ancient alder tree that grew in the middle of her home, and recited a calming spell. A shimmer of light appeared around her like a body halo, filling her with inner peace and strength.

She set off for Nix's cave.

"Who goes there?" asked a rumbly voice as the heavy slap of feet approached the front of the cave.

Cordelia gulped. Goblins weren't known for their hospitality. "It's Cordelia. I have an important matter to discuss with you."

"If it's about the witch's spell book, save your breath. I'm not giving it up."

"That book has been in her family for centuries. She wants it back."

"Ask me if I care. The feud between our kind has brewed far longer than that."

"Feud?"

"Long ago, the Witch of the Emerald Forest forbade goblins the right to use magical spells and wands, even though we're magical beings, too. I saw a chance to grab Juniper's spell book, and I took it. Now it's mine, and I'm not giving it back." If Nix's cave had a door, it would have slammed in Cordelia's face.

Cordelia, head lowered, approached Juniper's castle empty-handed.

"Well, where is it?" Juniper asked, leaning on her broomstick and wiping her brow.

"I'm working on it."

"I thought you cared about Selwyn." Juniper pulled herself up straight and glared at Cordelia.

Cordelia flinched.

"Off with you. Can't you see I'm busy ensuring the flowers bloom on time, the streams are crystal clear—all these mundane chores? It doesn't leave me time to properly protect and improve the forest."

Juniper's predicament gave Cordelia an idea. "What if I persuaded Nix to return your spell book in exchange for your allowing her to use a wand and perform magic?"

"What? It's forbidden."

"That was eons ago. You're the witch in charge now. I'm sure Nix would gladly be your assistant, allowing you to concentrate on more important issues."

Juniper perked up. "I suppose I could train her on simple spells. White magic only, mind you."

Cordelia breathed a sigh of relief. "I could make her a wand from a branch of my alder tree—"

"No! Absolutely not!"

Cordelia's face fell.

"No alder wood wand. That's for advanced practitioners of white and black magic." Juniper whispered the last two words. She opened a cupboard and retrieved a wand. "This is made from rowan wood. It's a protective wand that can never do evil. This will do for Nix."

"And my sister?"

"You'll have her back once the spell book is in my hands." She handed Cordelia the wand. "Take this. Tell Nix to show up here at dawn to begin her lessons." Juniper disappeared in a puff of smoke.

Cordelia hustled to Nix's cave. Nix's eyes latched onto the wand the moment Cordelia passed the threshold.

Nix strode toward Cordelia, one gnarled hand grabbing for the wand. "Give it to me."

"Not until I have the book."

"But Juniper will give me my own spell book, right?"

"Even better. She requested you join her at dawn to begin instruction. You'll learn wand magic from the most powerful witch in all witchdom."

The goblin stepped back, folding both arms in front of her. "What's the catch?"

"The catch?"

"Why is she suddenly being nice? Maybe there's a spell in this book for making gold. Perhaps I should hold on to it a little longer."

Selwyn didn't have a little longer. Cordelia thought fast and appealed to the goblin's vanity. "Don't tell her I told you so, but once you're trained in basic magic, you'll become her assistant and perform magic that keeps the forest safe and beautiful. That's an honor not bestowed on just anyone. All the forest creatures will look up to you."

Nix blinked her red eyes and smiled, displaying a row of yellowed fang-like teeth. "I can live with that." She handed Cordelia the spell book and clutched the wand to her chest.

Cordelia rushed through the forest to Juniper's dwelling. The witch was outside, tending to her magical herb garden, the late afternoon sun turning her hair to spun gold.

"I have your book," Cordelia said, waving it in the air with one hand like a wand.

Juniper reached for it, but Cordelia held it tight. "First, my sister—and your promise that you'll never blackmail me into doing your bidding again."

The witch shook her head. "Fairies are such a distrusting lot. But I promise, and you know I keep my word."

Juniper snapped her fingers and a beautiful butterfly landed on her hand. She waved her wand and Selwyn appeared. "Off with you now. I have work to do."

The two sisters embraced and then scampered away. At Cordelia's abode, over a pot of honey-sweetened chamomile tea, they discussed their experiences well into the wee hours of the morn.

"I never once doubted that you would save me," Selwyn concluded. "And look at all the good you did along the way. Everyone in the forest will benefit from Nix becoming Juniper's assistant. You're amazing."

Cordelia glowed under her sister's praise. "I don't know about that, but I think all will be well in the Emerald Forest for a long time to come."

# THE DELAY

## *Robert Runté*

"Damn." Milton jumped back as his coffee spilled off the counter and onto the floor. He looked around for the paper towels—which were never put back where they belonged—found them, tore off a handful of sheets which he dropped onto the floor and counter to soak up the spill.

"What's wrong?" his wife called from the other room.

"Oh, nothing. Just knocked my coffee over. I'll have to make another pot."

"You sound annoyed."

"It's just everything this morning," he complained. "I was hoping to hit the road early, and all these stupid, little, nothing things are slowing me down."

"Like what?" his wife's voice drifted in. He could picture her lying on the couch, knees up, laptop propped against her legs as she gave his kitchen drama the ten percent of her attention it warranted.

"Out of my shampoo, so had to go through the whole bathroom to find another bottle."

"You could have used mine," she said.

"And then," he said, ignoring the suggestion he should use her Rosemary-Mint volumizing shampoo, "I couldn't find my good suit—"

"Dry cleaners," she interrupted.

"—which I eventually remembered, but then the pants to the pinstripe didn't fit—"

"Not the pants' fault."

"—so I had to crawl into the basement cubby to get my winter suit out, but couldn't find the tie that goes with it—"

"Upstairs in the bedroom. You used it on the dog for Instagram."

"Oh yeah. I forgot about that." Milton smiled to himself. One of his better ones. "Anyway, I had to try on like five other ties before I found one that half-way matched or didn't have a stain, or whatever—"

"I've told you to always wash things before you put them away," she said.

"And now the coffee. It's going to make me ten minutes late at least."

"You could always skip the coffee."

"Seriously?"

He could feel her lifting her head from her work as she considered what he was like before his coffee. "No, I suppose not."

Whatever she said next was drowned out by the coffee grinder. He hadn't been able to find any ready-ground this morning, either.

"What?" he called, pouring the grounds into the percolator.

"I was going to suggest Starbucks drive-thru."

"There's always a lineup."

200

"Should have left more time, then," she said.

"More haste, less speed," he said back. "It's annoying."

It was annoying. He was annoyed. Though that could partly be attributed to the lack of coffee.

"It's just all these stupid little things at once," he said aloud. "Any one of them would have been okay, but all together they're going to make me late for the meeting. Like they can tell when you're in a hurry."

"That's right," his wife said, her tone telling him her attention was back on her laptop, "all your possessions are conspiring against you."

"Feels like it," he muttered. "Like they *want* me to be late."

"Or," his wife said, "the universe is trying to send you a message. Maybe being delayed ten minutes means the Humvee that runs a light and clobbers whatever is in the intersection, misses you and gets some other poor bastard. Maybe that coffee spill just saved your life."

"Yeah, sure." Milton said. "Something like that." He poured the new coffee into his travel mug, put the lid on, and went out to the car.

The garage door didn't work. He tried pressing the remote longer...then harder...then repeatedly. Then he got out of the car again so he could press the wall button, longer, harder, then repeatedly. Then he had to fetch a kitchen chair to climb up to disconnect the drive-chain so he could open it manually.

He backed the car out but had to stop again to close the garage. He hadn't meant to slam it down, but the door was effing heavy.

Still fuming, he drove out of the crescent and down the main road to join the inevitable lineup at the lights whenever one arrived later than 7:20.

In his head, he heard his wife's mocking, "First world problems..."

*Yeah,* he told himself, *I don't have cancer, my wife's awesome, my job's okay, and none of this crap matters.* He closed his eyes, took a deep breath, then a long, slow, deliberate sip of coffee. Starting the day over.

When there was no movement after the light cycled to red a second time, Milton opened his car door and stood on the edge of the seat to see what the hold-up was.

There was a Humvee blocking the intersection, and once he looked for it, he spotted the remains of a crumpled Ford Escort just peeking out over the edge of the ditch on the opposite side of the cloverleaf. A firetruck and an ambulance were coming up the far road.

Some of the cars ahead did a U-turn and rushed past him, no doubt seeking an alternate route to work. Milton remained where he was, staring at the Humvee with the crumpled bumper, as the cars ahead cleared from his view one by one.

Someone behind honked to bring Milton out of his trance, so he took his turn to drive back along the road to his crescent, parked out in his driveway, fished around for his house key, walked through to the kitchen and kissed the coffee pot he had earlier cursed.

"Forget something?" his wife called from the living room.

"Taking the day off," he said.

"I thought you had a meeting?"

"Got a message it wasn't that important," he said.

# Author's Bios

**Jill Hand** is the author of the Southern gothic thrillers, *White Oaks, Black Willows,* and *Red Pines.* Her work has appeared in many anthologies, most recently *Folk Horror,* from *Weird Fiction Quarterly.*

**Eddie Spohn** is a writer and horror fan from Long Island, New York. He can sometimes be found out on eastern Long Island painting homes for people with far more money than him. It's a life.

**Jonathan Reddoch** is co-owner of Collective Tales Publishing. He is a father, writer, editor, and publisher. He writes sci-fi, fantasy, romance, and especially horror. He's a prolific flash fiction author, but also writes poetry and short stories. He has been working on his enormous sci-fi novel for over a decade and would like to finish it in this lifetime if possible. He's from southern California, but lives in Salt Lake City. Notable works included in *Deluxe Darkness, Darkness 101: Lessons Were Learned,* and *This Isn't the Place.*

**Ed Ahern** resumed writing after forty odd years in foreign intelligence and international sales. He's had about 500 stories and poems published so far, and ten books. Ed works the other side of writing at *Bewildering Stories* where he manages a posse of seven review editors, and as lead editor at Scribes Micro.

**Rachel Dib** is a stay-at-home mom of three small children. After marrying a soldier, she left her home state of South Carolina to live in random places across the United States. Her short fiction appears in anthologies published by Havok Publishing, *Ye Olde Dragon Books, Iron Faerie* Publishing, Brigids Gate Press, and *The Last Line Literary Journal*. She also was awarded Havok's "Most Prolific Author" for 2022 and 2023.

**Teel James Glenn** has dozens of novels and stories published in over two hundred magazines including *Weird Tales, Cirsova, Black Cat Weekly, Mystery Magazine, Heroic Fantasy, Tough* and *Sherlock Holmes Mystery Magazine*. His novel *A Cowboy in Carpathia: A Bob Howard Adventure* won best novel 2021 in the Pulp Factory Award. *TheUrbanSwashbuckler.com* Facebook: Teel James Glenn

**Michael D. Burnside** earned a master's degree in political science at Ohio University but earns a living as a computer systems analyst. His fiction writing includes steampunk, science fiction, fantasy, and horror. His stories have been featured in multiple anthologies, including *Beautiful Lies, Painful Truths Vol. II, Ink Stains Vol. 8,* and *Dragon Gems*. His short stories have also been featured in magazines and podcasts such as *Devolution Z, Outposts of Beyond, Gathering Storm Magazine, Starship Sofa, Tall Tales TV,* and *Stupefying Stories*. Michael lives in Dayton, Ohio, with his wife, a giant dog, and lots of cats. Read more nice things about him, as well as some free stories, at https://mburnside3.wixsite.com/website.

**Paul Lonardo** is a freelance writer and author with numerous titles, both fiction and nonfiction books. Paul has placed short fiction and nonfiction articles in various genre magazines and ezines. He is a contributing writer for *Tales from the Moonlit Path* and an active HWA member.

**Douglas Goodell** published his first novel, "*Hiawatha and Beowulf.*" He's almost finished with the second book of the Hiawatha Saga. He's a former middle school teacher who grew up in Malden, Massachusetts. He's has been married to his wife, Melissa, for thirty-eight years and has three grown children.

**Reed Beebe** After years spent battling monsters and solving mysteries, Reed Beebe decided to become a writer. Reed's work has been published by AHOY Comics, DC Comics, and Soteira Press. Reed also blogs about comics at medium.com/meanwhile.

**Duncan Shepard** is a writer and musician living in Hartford, Connecticut. He began writing stories in 2022 as a way to connect with his late father. When not writing, Duncan creates music with his wife Chantelle in their band *The Striped Bananas.*

**Kevin Hopson's** work has appeared in a variety of anthologies, magazines, and e-zines, and he enjoys writing in multiple genres. You can learn more about Kevin by visiting his website at http://www.kmhopson.com.

**James Austin McCormick is** a college lecturer from the rainy city of Manchester (UK) and also a part time writer of speculative fiction, mainly sci-fi, horror and sword and sorcery fantasy. Where possible he likes to blend these genres together. For me, writing is all about escapism and world building. The more he can remove my stories from the mundane, day to day world, the more he enjoy writing them. IJames has been writing for twenty years or so and has been fortunate enough to have had several short stories and novellas published in various anthologies as well as some short novels published by *Class Act Books*. You can find most (not quite all) of his published works at the following link:

https://isfdb.org/cgi-bin/ea.cgi?195589

**Joe Stout** is an east Tennessee based writer who focuses on short stories and flash fiction. His work has been published by the *Non-Binary Review, Every Day Fiction,* and *CafeLit.* When he's not writing, he enjoys exploring the mountains and spending time with his children. You can follow him on Facebook at Joe Stout Writing or Instagram @joestoutwriting.

**Bethany W. Pope** has won many literary awards and published several novels and collections of poetry. Nicholas Lizard, writing for *The Guardian,* described Bethany's latest book as 'poetry as salvation'....'This harrowing collection drawn from a youth spent in an orphanage delights in language as a place of private escape.' Bethany currently lives and works in China.

**Gregg Chamberlain** writes speculative fiction for fun, and zombie filk because he can. He has several dozen examples of both in various magazines and anthologies. He lives in quiet, but productive, retirement in rural Ontario, Canada, with his missus, Anne, and their cats, who think that belly rubs and treats should be available at all times without asking.

**Andrew Kurtz** is an up-and-coming horror author who writes very graphic and violent short stories which have appeared in numerous horror anthologies. Since childhood, he has loved horror films and literature. His favorite authors are Stephen King, Clive Barker, H.G. Wells, Richard Matheson, Edgar Rice Boroughs, and Ian Fleming. https://linktr.ee/horror672

**Kyla Chapek** is a thirty-five-year-old woman living in Redmond, Washington and identifies with the LGBTQ community. Kyla grew up in McKenzie River, Oregon and graduated from McKenzie High School and Oregon State University. She is a former member of the Wordos Critique group based in Eugene, and Willamette Writers group. She sails the culinary seas as a manager at Trader Joe's by day and creates new worlds with the stroke of her keyboard by night. Kyla dreams of the time writing becomes her day and night job. When she is not reading or writing, Kyla enjoys training in martial arts, traveling and getting lost in the woods with her dog. Some of Kyla's previously published work can be found in *Bards and Sages Magazine*, *Silver Blade Magazine*, and *Fantasia Divinity Magazine*.

**John Frochio** lives in Western Pennsylvania and recently retired from developing and supporting computer automation systems for steel mills and hospitals. He's had stories published in various online publications and anthologies, including *Triangulation: Parch* (2014), *Time Travel Tales* (2016), *Visions VII: Universe* (2017), 2047: Short Stories from *Our Common Future* (2017), The *Chronos Chronicles* (2018), T*hird Flatiron's Hidden Histories* (2019), *Something Wicked This Way Rides* (2021), S*trange Aeon: Orbital Lovecraft* (2021), *Strange Wars* (2022), and *Legion Press* (2023). His wife Connie, a retired nurse, and his daughter Toni, a flight attendant, have bravely put up with his strange ways for many years. His author's webpage is https://johnafrochio.wordpress.com/about/.

**S. Cameron David** A longtime resident of New York state, has had a love of all things fantasy and folklore for as long as he can remember. When he isn't dreaming of traveling long lost roads into Faerie, you can find him online at https://scamerondavid.wordpress.com/

**Pamela Love** was born in New Jersey. After graduating from Bucknell University and working as a teacher and in marketing, she turned to writing. Her fiction has also appeared in the anthologies *Happy Holiday Historicals, Legendary: Havok Season Ten,* and *Wyrms: An Anthology of Dragon Drabbles,* among other publications. She lives in Maryland.

**Garry Engkent**, Chinese-Canadian, has taught at various colleges and universities. He has co-authored three texts: *Groundwork: Writing Skills to Build On; Fiction/Non-*

*Fiction: A Reader and Rhetoric, 2ⁿᵈ ed.*; and *Essay: Do's and Don'ts, 3ʳᵈ ed.* His stories have appeared in *Exile, Many-Mouthed Birds, Ricepaper Magazine*, etc. Most stories have a Chinese immigrant slant, circa 1950-70s: "Why My Mother Can't Speak English,""Visiting". "Eggroll", "Acceptance" and "Rabbit". He has branched out to horror: "*I, Zombie: A Different Point of View*, "*The Zombie and the Shedim*," and "*Merci*" among others.

**Mike Murphy** has had over 150 audio plays produced in the U.S. and overseas. He's won The Columbine Award and a dozen *Moondance* International Film Festival awards in their TV pilot, audio play, short screenplay, and short story categories. His prose has appeared in many magazines and anthologies. In 2020, his screenplay *Die Laughing* was a semi-finalist in the Unique Voices Screenplay Competition from *Creative Screenwriting Magazine*. The following year, his TV pilot script "The Bullying Squad" was a quarter-finalist in the *Emerging Writers* Genre Screenplay Competition. Mike is the writer of two short films, *Dark Chocolate* and *Hotline*. In 2013, he won the inaugural Marion Thauer Brown Audio Drama Scriptwriting Competition. In 2020, he came in second. For several of the in-between years, he served as a judge. Mike keeps a blog at audioauthor.blogspot.com.

**Jeanna Mason Stay** is a sucker for fairy tales, fantasy, and romantic comedies, so she especially likes it when they go together. She also loves fireflies, serial commas, birds of paradise, and galahs. She dreams of one day owning a herd of Chia sheep. Jeanna is currently happily-ever-aftering with her handsome husband, four charming children, and zero pets (if you don't count all the rocks) in Utah. She misses the bright skies and red rock of Alice Springs, Australia. Find her (very) occasionally on Facebook @JeannaMasonStay or on Instagram @jeanna.mason.stay.

**Tom Folsk**e lives in Minnesota with his wife, four kids, and three black cats. He has had over 30 short stories published or in the process of being published, with new stories to be featured in upcoming projects by British Fantasy Society, *Theaker Quarterly Fiction*, *Dark Moon Rising Publications*, and *House of Loki Press*. See more at https://tfolske1987.wixsite. com/mysite

**Guy Belleranti** writes fiction, nonfiction, poetry and more for adults and children. His work has been published by over 230 different publications including *Mystery Magazine*, *Scifaikuest*, *parABnormal Magazine*, *Woman's World*, *Highlights for Children*, *Humpty Dumpty magazine* and many educational publishers for children. His author website is guy-belleranti.weebly.com.

**Claire Davon**, a U SA Today Bestselling author has written for most of her life, starting with fan fiction when she was very young. She writes across a wide range of genres, and does not consider any of it off limits. Her novels can be found in the paranormal romance and contemporary romance sections, while her short stories run the gamut. If a story calls to her, she will write it. She currently lives in Los Angeles and spends her free time writing novels and short stories, as well as doing animal rescue and enjoying the sunshine. Claire's website is www.clairedavon.com.

**D. Thomas Minton** is the author of the *Calypto Cycle*, a series of espionage thrillers set in an alternative 1920s eastern Europe and the middle east. His short fiction has appeared in many publications, including *Asimov's, Apex*, and *Lightspeed* Magazines. He lives, works, and writes from his home in the mountains of British Columbia, Canada, but his idle musings can be found holding court at dthomasminton.com.

**Albert N. Katz** (he/him), after 43 years as a cognitive scientist, retired from academia, and started a new career as a writer of short stories and poetry. His stories and poems have appeared since in anthologies, genre-based (detective, horror, and science fiction) and literary magazines. His story, *Hocus-Pocus*, is a past winner of the Flash Fiction competition sponsored by Kansas City Voices/Whispering Prairie Press. His poem "Cracked Boulders" was one of the winners in the 2023 Polar Express National Poetry Contest and his poem "Along the Saint John River" was awarded a Special judges prize in the Drummond Poetry Competition (2024). He can be reached at: Albert Katz, 7-634 Brunswick St., Fredericton, NB. CANADA E3B 1H6 or visit psychkatz@yahoo.com

**Lana Nizhehorodova** is from Odesa, Ukraine. Her fiction appeared in Variety Pack, The Temz Review as well as the anthology *"Digital Love"* by Dragon Soul Press. For Lana, writing is something that brings her a great deal of enjoyment and she hopes her work will be enjoyable for you to read too.

**Steven Streeter** is from rural Australia and has been writing since childhood. He is a former professional wrestler, with two children, and has recently completed his third university degree. An unabashed fan of pulp fiction and escapist entertainment, he has had a number of short stories published in anthologies. He has also had a young adult horror novella published (*Under Ground*, Black Hare Press), and two adult horror novels (*Patch of Green*, Little Demon Books; *Invasive Species*, AM Ink).

**Conrad Gardner's** writing has appeared in Superlative Literary Journal, AutoFocus, and Sci Phi Journal. When not writing, he can be found running, reading, watching, and dreaming of a better, brighter tomorrow.

**Anne Karppinen** is a university teacher, musician and writer based in Finland. In addition to a PhD in Contemporary Culture, she hold a M.A. in English, and did Creative Writing in the UK as a part of her studies. She's been teaching writing – both academic and creative – for over ten years now. My short stories have appeared in e.g. *Not One of Us, Mirror Dance* and *Impossible Worlds*. "The Lamplighter's Daughter" was chosen for the *Best of Wyldblood* anthology in 2022. Her book, *The Songs of Joni Mitchell*, was published by Routledge.

**DJ Tyrer** dwells on the northern shore of the Thames estuary, close to the world's longest pleasure pier in the decaying seaside resort of Southend-on-Sea, and is the person behind Atlantean Publishing. *Sir Blodry* has previously appeared in stories published in *Eeny Meeny Miney Mo* (Patchwork Raven), *Tournament Games* (Zimbell House Publishing), a*nd an issue of Tigershark* ezine, as well as on Frostfire Words. DJ Tyrer has also had work published in such places as Mrs *Claus* (Worldweaver Press) and issues of *Fantasia Divinity, Broadswords and Blasters*, BFS Horizons, and *The Fifth D*i. DJ Tyrer's website is at

https://djtyrer.blogspot.co.uk/ DJ Tyrer's Facebook page is at https://www.facebook.com/DJTyrerwriter/

The Atlantean Publishing website is at https://atlanteanpublishing.wordpress.com/

**Tom Howard** is a science fiction and fantasy short story writer with almost one hundred and fifty short stories sold. He lives in Little Rock, Arkansas, USA and retired from working around the world as a banking software consultant. He has four children who, along with his grandson, provide him with many story ideas. He's had careers in the US Air Force working as a communications analyst for NSA and as a Titan missile officer. He was employed in corporate America as a technical writer and an analyst for financial systems. He founded the Central Arkansas Speculative Fiction Writers' Group for local writers and is the moderator for Spinners, an online speculative fiction critique group on Inked Voices. Originally from the South Bend, Washington, Tom has lived in Germany, England, Japan, Australia, Hong Kong, and the Philippines. Tom publishes his sold short stories in anthologies available on Amazon: *Collected Science Fiction, Volume 1, Collected Fantasy, Volume* 1, and *Superworld Stories, Volume 1.*

He's currently working on volume 2 versions of each of the anthologies. He's also working on several novels, including book three of his *Three Desert Roses* epic fantasy and book three of his Aurora space opera series.

**Michael Haynes** is an avid short fiction reader and writer with nearly 100 published stories, most in the speculative fiction genres. He lives in Colorado and has more hobbies than he really has time for, enjoying travel, going to concerts, photography, cooking, geocaching, hiking, board games, and so on. His debut short fiction collection is *AT THE INTERSECTION OF LOVE AND DEATH.* Learn more at his website michaelhaynes.info.

**Magnolia Silcox** is a Schizophrenic bisexual twenty-one year old author from Vicksburg,Mississippi. Her hobbies include writing, sewing, and watching anime. In her free time she sews dolls for kids in hospitals and refugee camps. She is also into theater and acting in several different plays within her community theater guild. She lives with her parents,younger sister and two little brothers. She is also an animal lover with one bird and two cats. She enjoys writing about Schizophrenic and bisexual people just like her.

**Dawn DeBraal** lives in rural Wisconsin with her husband, a stray cat and a rescued dog. She has published over 600 short stories, drabbles, and poems in online ezines and anthologies. She tends to lean toward the horror genre because it makes her life seem so much better! *Falling Star Magazine* nominated *Dawn* for the 2019 Pushcart Award; she was Runner-up in the 2022 Horror Story Competition, two-time Author of the

Month, nominated 2020, 2022, 2023 Author of the Year and received Contributor of the Year 2023 *Spillwords Magazine*. https://www.facebook.com/All-The-Clever-Names-Were-Taken-114783950248991 https://linktr.ee/dawndebraal

**Maureen Bowden** is a Liverpudlian, living with her musician husband in North Wales. She has had over 200 stories and poems accepted by paying markets including Third Flatiron, Water Dragon Publishing, The First Line and many others. She was nominated for the 2015 international Pushcart Prize and in 2019 Hiraeth Books published an anthology of her stories, *Whispers of Magic*. They plan to publish an anthology of her poetry in the near future. She also writes song lyrics, mostly comic political satire, set to traditional melodies and her husband has performed them in folk music clubs throughout the UK. She loves her family and friends, rock 'n' roll, Shakespeare, and cats.

**L.N. Hunter's** comic fantasy novel, *The Feather and the Lamp* (Three Ravens Publishing), sits alongside works in anthologies such as *Best of British Science Fiction 2022* and *Hidden Villains: Arise*, as well as several issues of Short Édition's *Short Circuit* and the *Horrifying Tales of Wonder* podcast. There have also been papers in the IEEE *Transactions on Neural Networks*, which are probably somewhat less relevant and definitely less entertaining. When not writing, L.N. occasionally masquerades as a software developer or can be found unwinding in a disorganised home in Carlisle, UK, along with two cats and a soulmate. https://linktr. ee/l.n.hunter https://www.facebook.com/L.N.Hunter.writer

**Christopher J. Burke** is a writer, creator of the webcomic *x, why?*, and math teacher from Brooklyn. He cowrote GURPS Autoduel, 2nd edition for Steve Jackson Games and has appeared in Mad Magazine. A collection of his stories, *In A Flash* 2020, was published by eSpec Books. A second collection, A Bucket Full of Moonlight, is coming out in September 2024. His stories have appeared in *Daily Science Fiction, MetaStellar*, and *Science Fiction Lampoon*, and in the anthology *Devilish & Divine.*He's currently publishing a series of short fiction books called *Burke's Lore Brief*s. His website is http://mrburkemath.net.

**Helen Liptak** has written over twenty young adult comedy/dramas, published numerous short stories and flash fiction, and completed five books. Currently in the midst of creating a series of standalone but interrelated Regency Romances about vicars and viscounts, Ms. Liptak's Regencies have won awards in the FHL contest for unpublished writers, the 2023 Foundations Award at BRMCWC, while her YA novel placed third in the Blue Ridge Foundations Award in 2024. After extensive travel immersed in middle school culture for more years than she would care to mention, she now weaves her stories in South Carolina.

**Dawn Colclasure** is a writer in Oregon. She is a freelance writer, columnist and book reviewer. She is the author and co-author of several books. Her work has appeared in newspapers, magazines, anthologies and websites. Her websites are https://dawnsbooks.com/ and https://www.dmcwriter.com/. Her X is @dawnwilson325 and her insta is dawn10325.

**Rhys Hughes** was born in Wales but has lived in many different countries. He began writing at an early age and his first book, Worming the Harpy, was published in 1995. Since that time he has published more than fifty other books and his work has been translated into ten languages. He recently completed an ambitious project that involved writing exactly 1000 linked short stories. He is currently working on a novel and several new collections of prose and verse.

**C Lenz** is a writer, scientist, and odd little thing. Her stories have been published by Metaphorosis, the NoSleep Podcast, and Fairfield MicroScribes, as well as others, and her debut novella Thyrst Festival will be released November 15th, 2024. She lives in Hamilton, Ontario, Canada with her wife Thana.

**Shari Held** is an Indianapolis-based, award-winning fiction author who spins tales of fantasy, crime, mystery, romance, and horror. More than forty of her short stories have been published in a variety of magazines and anthologies, including *Hoosier Noir, Yellow Mama, Trees* by Jersey Pines Ink, *Trick or Treats - Tales of All Hallows' Eve*, and *Tales of the Sea*. Visit her website—www.shariheld.com—to find out more about her and her stories.

**Robert Runté** is Senior Editor with EssentialEdits. ca where he edits SF&F. A retired professor, he has three aurora Awards for his literary criticism, is currently a reviewer with *The Ottawa Review of Books* and serves on the Editorial Advisory Board of Shadowpaw Press. His own short fiction has been published over 100 times. He is married, has two adult daughters, four dogs, and a bad hip.